Birds in the Rain

Praise for *Birds in the Rain*

Rana Hanna writes with the precision of a photographer and the heart of a poet. Through Layla's lens, Marc's quiet endurance, Jeddo's generational sorrow, and Michael's moral awakening, Hanna captures not just what is seen but what is deeply felt. Each character is framed like a photograph: vivid, intimate, and unforgettable. Her storytelling is as composed as a portrait, yet alive with the raw light of human truth.

— *Ihab Ismail*

A beautiful and deeply human book. *Birds in the Rain* delicately touches on the themes of life we intuitively know matter most, yet are often difficult to express: loss, love, and the indifference of circumstance. How the banality of the everyday contrasts with the wonder of dreaming.

War-torn Beirut is the stage. But this book is not a love letter to Lebanon, and all the stories that shape it. It is, to me, a life letter, one that elegantly captures the emotional complexity of those who call that country home.

— **Antonio Hanna-Amodio**

What a lovely, gripping, well-written novel. I enjoyed every bit of it. Well done! I laughed my head off.

I felt joy, sadness, love, and hatred while reading; I cried on several pages. I lived each chapter with Layla, Jeddo, Michael and Marc.

Rana is a brilliant writer. It is a book that will be on my library bookshelf.

— *Bassem Abdulrahim*

The story is very engaging! The beginning of the story is captivating and immediately drew me in. I found myself needing to keep reading to find out whether Michael is still alive. The characters have depth, and I love how the author moves between past and present so we understand them better.

The themes that stood out to me the most were the deep love for our country despite its ongoing struggles with war and corruption, as well as the longing to return home. The descriptions of familiar places and foods like manousheh and Turkish coffee make the story feel incredibly immersive.

The description of Marc returning to his parents' home and touching the furniture as he recalled his childhood brought me to tears. I do that whenever I visit my grandmother's house.

Birds in the Rain is a fantastic read!
—*Bianca Chalfoun*

Amazing book. I loved it. It brought back so many memories, good and bad, and so many feelings, nice and not so nice. Thank you, Rana, for writing it.

—*Aline Hobeika Papachristoforou*

I've been carrying the book with me ever since I finished reading it. I was so moved—completely in love with the story of Michael, Marc, Layla, and Jeddo and the way the author wove their lives together with such tenderness and complexity.

Rana captured the ache and beauty of coming of age through four distinct characters, each so richly drawn, each holding pain, hope, and depth. I was in awe of how, in such a short span of pages, she gave them all a path to redemption—I could go on and on!
—*Laura Barr*

A NOVEL

Birds
in the
Rain

Rana Hanna

BOLD
STORY
PRESS

CHEVY CHASE, MARYLAND

Bold Story Press, Chevy Chase, MD 20815
www.boldstorypress.com

Note: On page xi, "'Hope' is the thing with feathers" by
Emily Dickinson appeared in Dickinson's assembled
Fascicle Thirteen, Sheet Two.

First edition: August 2025
Library of Congress Control Number: 2025902790
ISBN: 978-1-954805-74-3 (paperback)
ISBN: 978-1-954805-75-0 (e-book)

Cover and interior design by KP Books

Printed in the United States of America
10   9   8   7   6   5   4   3   2   1

———

For my boys.

And for Tanya
You believed in me, and I didn't
have the heart to let you down.

———

Today's incident is between the State of Israel and
Lebanon. As to where to attack, the moment that the
state of Lebanon is involved, everything is legitimate and
it's important to know that. Everything is legitimate.

MAJOR GENERAL UDI ADAM, JULY 12, 2006

Those who do not remember the past
are condemned to repeat it.

GEORGE SANTAYANA

"Hope" is the thing with feathers –
That perches in the soul –
And sings the tune without the words –
And never stops – at all –

And sweetest – in the Gale – is heard –
And sore must be the storm –
That could abash the little Bird
That kept so many warm –

I've heard it in the chillest land
And on the strangest Sea –
Yet – never – in Extremity,
It asked a crumb – of me.

EMILY DICKINSON

Prologue

Today is the twelfth of July, 2006. This morning, Hezbollah fighters in Southern Lebanon attacked two armored tanks patrolling the Israeli side of the border fence and abducted two Israeli soldiers. Another three were killed in the ambush. The Israeli Defense Forces promised massive retaliation if the soldiers are not returned by midnight.

Today, just six weeks shy of my sixteenth birthday, I will go missing. Sort of. Things aren't always as they seem. "It's not the cat," as my mother likes to say. "It's never the cat."

Layla

Layla stared at the plate of chocolate macaroons. She still wasn't convinced. She moved the board in front of the window a few inches to the right. There.

The man on the video recorder was saying: "It's the way you approach objects that may not be necessarily naturally beautiful or desirable, but the light reflecting off them makes them so. Move your body and see how the light is playing off different objects."

"Drama!" her editor had said. "Give me drama. I want people shaken to their core when they see these images."

"If you want drama," Layla had answered, "then send me to the street, don't give me a box of macaroons."

"Well, as it happens, we are a life*style* magazine, not *Life* magazine."

Later, he'd texted her asking her if she was busy that night.

"Yes," she'd texted back. "I'm seeing your wife."

Layla fastened the camera on the camera stand and peered through the viewfinder. The man on the screen was making food photography sound like opera.

"Chocolate is so emotional for people: catching just the glimp—" And with that he was gone. The fan stopped whirring, and Layla guessed that the electricity had cut. She checked her watch. Noon. Bang on time. Luckily, she didn't need any artificial light, but if she were going to suffer through the July heat in Beirut, she might as well be in her darkroom.

She braced herself for the silence and the darkness.

In her darkroom, a converted storage cupboard, Layla engaged in her two favorite activities: developing and regret. On this particular July twelfth morning in 2006, the heat and humidity were so high that Layla felt the sweat beads slide down her back almost as soon as she moved. The trays and the enlarger took up all the available room. From one wall to the next ran a string on which she hung the developed pictures to dry. She could only fit two or three at a time, and so her forays into this private, tiny world of hers were short and frequent.

Her eye twitched constantly. As she clipped the A4-sized paper into one tray full of liquid and then dipped it into another, she tried to keep her hand steady. She felt palpitations in her chest and sweat beads on her forehead. She carefully immersed the paper into the tray with the fixer. As she waited for one image to appear, she tried to dismiss another from her mind: That of her son walking out the door earlier that day, head bowed, backpack hanging casually from his shoulder. He had looked back at her, and she couldn't quite read his expression, a combination of sadness and pity perhaps.

Layla carefully removed the now developed photo from the fixer liquid and hung it up to dry. The girl looked back at her with piercing, defiant eyes. She stood with her short, thin legs splayed, the roses she carried almost as tall as she, her clothes tattered and dirty. "What's your story, little girl?" Layla asked. "Tell me yours, and I'll tell you mine."

Her butt cheek buzzed, but she ignored it. It was probably Michael calling to apologize—again. This time she would not answer. This time he would need to learn that he could not throw his anger at her and leave, that he could not turn his back on her mid-sentence, that he could not just ignore her.

And there it was, the regret. Maybe if she had been gentler, calmer. Maybe if she had listened more and shouted less. Maybe if she hadn't kicked the printer or thrown his shoe at the AC vent. Maybe if she had been more collected, as she remembered her mother had been. Maybe if she had been the kind of person Sebastian had been, or more like Michael. If she were to be truly honest with herself, Michael hadn't actually walked out on her mid-sentence this morning; she had kicked him out.

"Go!" she had screamed. "Go before I say or do something I'll truly regret. But find a place to stay tonight, because you're not coming back to this house!"

"Okay," he said. Simple. Concise. She hated that about him. She could swear he had grown taller since the day before, but his face still held on to its baby fat, the angles on his jaw and cheeks just beginning to fight for space.

At that moment she wanted to run to him and hug him, to beg him to stay, beg him to forgive her, again, never to leave her. Instead, she simply said, "Maybe your *Jeddo* can help, or Marc."

"Okay."

What she really resented about her relationship with Michael, what really drove her to the end of her wits, was his maturity and his calmness. The boy was only sixteen, almost, and seemed to grasp the world with so much assurance and confidence, so much knowledge and wisdom, that she often wondered who was the parent and who was the child. She wondered what Sebastian would have thought of him. As images of father and child projected in her head, she cried. She let the salty droplets linger at the edge of her mouth for a moment.

Layla reached for the phone in her back pocket. It had stopped buzzing. She flipped it open and saw one missed call from Marc and one message. She heard the home phone ringing, but Michael never called the home phone; he always called her on her mobile, so she didn't bother to answer.

The pictures had dried, and she unpinned them from the line. The magazines and the ad agencies loved her work, the gallerists less so. "You're too safe," one bald man in his forties with thick dark glasses had told her. "Maybe if you got out of your comfort zone a bit." She wanted to ask him if he knew that he looked like a typical gallerist and if it was by chance or by design. "Maybe," he continued, "maybe if you went out when everybody turned in, that's when you'd see the city you're trying so hard to depict."

"I do go out when everyone turns in," she had said. "But it's not to take pictures."

Her phone buzzed again, and when she saw it was Marc, she ignored it.

She flapped her arms wildly in the small cupboard she had turned into her darkroom, trying to shake off the anxiety. Her doctor had suggested she get a dog.

"You won't believe the therapeutic benefits of petting a dog," he had said.

"I don't have time for a dog," she had answered.

Here it comes again.

"Mama, calm down, please!" Michael had pleaded with her.

"Can't stand this heat," she had muttered as she kicked the printer.

"What? Can't stand the ink either?" Michael had asked. That's when she had kicked him out.

She shut her eyes tight. Pull yourself together, Layla.

"Go!" she had screamed. "Quickly. Get out before I say or do something I'll regret." The last time she had said that, to Sebastian, he hadn't returned. Maybe the same might happen to Michael.

"We're not born suspicious," she said to the image of the unkempt street girl. "Experience makes us so. Living with fear and uncertainty makes us so."

She pulled the next picture from the liquid in the tray marked *Fixer* and hung it up to dry.

Layla checked her watch to see how much time she could still afford to spend in the darkroom before she had to start setting up the second shoot for the day. She was relieved to be in her darkroom. The darkroom always calmed her down. Maybe it was the darkness, or the silence, or the fact that she was so concentrated on her craft. She was very meticulous, often printing an image over and over again until she managed to obtain the exact shades of gray she was after. She enjoyed the process, loved seeing her stories take shape and come to life. She never tired of it, even though she had done it hundreds of times. In the race for supremacy between words and images, she sided with the one as opposed to the many.

Her darkroom allowed her to escape the world outside. Beirut was noisy with traffic; vegetable and fruit vendors were selling their produce, causing even more traffic and honking horns, neighbors shouting to each other across balconies above the din of the streets below. It was a scene more befitting a 1950s southern Italian film set than a capital city. She felt enveloped and protected in her makeshift space. In that small cupboard there was no evil, no war, no goodbye. There were no words, no acceptance letters to her son from prestigious institutions 3,000 miles away, no cards expressing sadness and condolences at the passing of her husband. There were no sirens in the middle of the night, no phone call sending her to lawyers' meetings or delivering news of yet another death or explosion. In the darkroom there were no random bombs killing a prominent journalist or politician as there had been over the past few years in Beirut. There was only the red light and the whirring of the fan, when there was electricity.

But today, even the darkness and the silence did not seem to comfort her. She blamed the heat. It was hot in the converted storage cupboard, especially in Beirut in July. She checked her watch again. She really had to get to work. Almost two in the afternoon, too early for a glass of wine. Maybe a cigarette was what she needed.

Back at her workstation, her phone blinked. It was Marc. She ignored it. It stopped and immediately started blinking again. This time it wouldn't let up.

"Is Michael with you?" Marc asked.

"No," she stood shock still. "Why?"

Here it comes again.

"Where is he?" Marc asked.

"At the beach. Why?"

"We agreed to meet. At twelve, he . . ." Marc caught himself mid-sentence. He didn't see the point in making her panic and setting her off.

"Why are you panting? What's wrong? What's going on?!" Layla asked.

Here it comes again.

"Listen. There's nothing wrong. Yet. Just go pick him up. Or just tell me which beach he's at. I'll go."

"No. No. I'll go. Tell me what's going on. What do you mean he didn't show up? Show up where?" Layla insisted.

Here it comes again.

8   BIRDS IN THE RAIN

"I'll explain later. Some militiamen have attacked the Israeli border, and now the Israelis are pissed off. They're threatening to attack."

Here it comes again.

"What're you saying?" Layla asked.

Marc could sense his pulse rising. Layla's stubbornness exasperated him. He could just see her wide eyes, deep and troubled like the sea after a wild storm, looking at him, uncomprehending. And instead of a stubborn, mature woman, all he could see was a scared child. Marc sighed. "They've abducted two Israeli soldiers, and the Israelis are threatening to raze this country to the ground if they're not returned by midnight tonight. I really don't think he should be out there at this time."

"Ok, I'm going."

Here it comes again. Here it comes again. Here it comes again.

———

Layla drove with her hand close to the horn, like her friend Zeina had taught her all those years ago. It was necessary, Zeina had explained, to navigate the clogged streets of the city. When Layla had returned to Beirut, Zeina had picked her up from the airport. A highway was being built, hell the whole country was being built after a devastating fifteen-year war. The tally would come to 150,000 dead, but during that moment in the early 1990s, as they navigated the busy streets that led from the airport in the southern suburbs to the inner city, they had to contend with too many cars on too few roads, chickens vying with pedestrians for street-crossing space, and donkeys taking up what was left of the crumbling sidewalk. The air had smelled of burning trash.

"Not your average tourist postcard," Layla had remarked from the back seat as she closed her window. The heat had been suffocating, but it beat the deafening noise and the intoxicating smells. She had unwrapped the blanket around the infant cradled in her arms. In a country fresh out of civil war, where hospitals were still counting mutilated limbs and families were still searching for their missing loved ones, car seats were the least of people's concerns.

Now, fifteen years later, she was halfway to the beaches of Jiyeh, just twenty kilometers south of the city. The roads were empty going south, the Lebanese having perfected the art of scurrying off the streets as soon as they heard the siren of an ambulance, the echo of a bomb, or more simply the ping of a phone announcing news of an assassination, a drive-by shooting, or a kidnapping. It was like an anvil landing in a flock of pigeons in a busy square, a perfectly choreographed response to trauma.

She switched on the radio.

The attack killed two Israeli soldiers and wounded seven, the voice on the radio said.

She thought of Zeina. Where was she now? She hadn't spoken to her childhood friend since Zeina had checked herself out of rehab again. Layla felt guilty that she had lost touch, but she had to protect herself. She had to protect Michael. Zeina had not tried to contact her either. Layla had often compared herself to her friend, wondered who had suffered more from the civil war—those who left, like her, or those who stayed. For those who had stayed, so much violence needed to be forgotten, and there were so many drugs to help alleviate the pain. War money was easy money, more easily dispensed with for the sake of pain relief. And for the fifteen years between 1975 and 1990, there had been a lot of war in Beirut.

*Israel's prime minister Ehud Olmert said the attack was
an act of war by Lebanon.*

That day in the car, her first day back in almost ten years,
Zeina had asked her:

"You know who are the real winners of the war, Layla?
The Syrians. Look, they're everywhere." They had been
stopped at a Syrian army checkpoint and, despite the fact
that there had been nothing suspicious about two women
in a car with a baby, the young soldier had still poked his
head uncomfortably close through the driver window to
take a better look before waving them off.

Mr. Olmert has said he holds Lebanon responsible . . .

"Are you sure you want to move back here?" Zeina had
asked, clearing her lungs from the soldier's stinking breath.
"Why would anyone choose to leave the navel of the world
only to settle in its butthole?"

. . . and that it would pay a heavy price.

"I need to start again," Layla had answered. "And this
butthole is my home."

"Let's see for how long," Zeina had replied.

*The prime minister has called an emergency meeting but
has already ruled out negotiations.*

Layla tried calling Michael again but couldn't get through.
The phone lines were clogging under pressure. People would
be calling each other. Layla cursed every fifteen-year-old
on the planet for being so irresponsible. Hadn't he and his
friends heard what was going on? Why had he not called her?

*Israeli ground troops have entered southern Lebanon
to search for the two soldiers for the first time since Israel
ended its occupation of South Lebanon six years ago.*

Sure, Layla thought, after it had been deemed by the
Israeli government that too many of its soldiers had been
killed by homemade bombs hung, like lemons, in roadside
trees. Murderous fruit.

Two civilians were killed when Israeli planes bombed a road bridge . . .

She tried Michael again.

Civilians in northern Israel have been told to stay in their shelters.

She pressed harder on the gas pedal and kept her hand closer to the horn.

Fifteen minutes and countless banana plantations later, Layla finally turned off the coastal highway and veered onto the gravelly, dusty road that would lead her to the beach club where Michael was. They were closing up, and the bathers stood waiting outside as if watching a procession for the valet to bring their cars or for someone to pick them up. None of this lot seemed worried as they clutched their Gucci beach bags. Just another day at the office. She could hear bombing in the distance, and her stomach churned. She stepped out of her car and scouted the various heads. She spotted Michael's friends, but her son was not among them.

"Boys?" Layla asked. "Where's Michael?" She could hardly breathe, despite the hot July wind slapping her hair and her face.

"Oh, hi, Layla!" said the blondish one, Patrick, while the others all shrugged in perfect sync, almost as if they had been rehearsing all morning.

"Where's Michael?" she reached behind Patrick's back and took the cigarette from his hand.

"You shouldn't smoke," she said. "It's bad for you." She took a drag from the cigarette before she threw it to the ground.

"Michael?"

"Yes, Michael! Who else could I be looking for? He said he was coming to the beach with you guys."

Patrick just shook his head. Layla had known him since he was almost two years old and was very fond of him, but on this particular occasion, she could imagine unwinding his braces and jolting him awake with the wire. She held him by the shoulders.

"Patrick? Where is he?"

"I dunno." He shuffled the ground with his feet. "He didn't come with us here. He stayed in the taxi and went off somewhere. He wouldn't say."

Here it comes again.

"What aren't you telling me, Patrick?" Layla edged in closer to him, squeezing his shoulder a bit too hard.

"I don't know, Layla," Patrick whimpered. "I really don't. He said something about a hike, but I had my music on. I didn't hear, I swear!"

"What hike?" She looked at the other boys. They were all staring at their feet.

"Do you boys know anything?"

Again, the rehearsed chorus. She let go of Patrick, and they all scampered to the waiting Range Rover a few cars back.

The valet came screaming at her to remove her car from the middle of the road. Suddenly she heard cars honking behind her. She held her flying hair back from her face as she tried to unscramble her mind and think clearly. She could almost hear it clanking.

Here it comes again.

Layla sat in her car. Clank, clank, clank. She looked out her car window. Where are you, Michael? Where are you? Where did you go? Why did you go? Why did you go, Sebastian? Where did you go, Sebastian? Where did you go? Why did you go? Don't worry. Don't worry. I'll be right back. I'll be right back.

Jeddo

Layla walked into her flat in the Badaro district of Beirut to find her father waiting for her in the hallway.

"Marc called me," he said. He looked beyond her shoulder. "Where's Michael?"

Layla stared blankly at him.

He knew that look. It was the same look he had seen when she picked him up from the airport for Sebastian's funeral. It was the look he had seen when he walked into their home after spending three sleepless nights at the hospital tending to his own wife all those years ago.

He led her into the kitchen and sat her down at the table. As he rummaged around, Layla stared quietly at the Beirut rooftops with their rusty metallic water tanks juxtaposed against rooftops with swimming pools and palm trees, a jumble of old and new, rich and poor. It would have been interesting had it not been so ugly. He placed a cup of sweet tea and a tumbler of bourbon on the table in front of her and went into the living room. He knew, at moments like these, to leave his daughter alone and to be as quiet as possible.

On the street below, nothing moved. No cars, no horns, no prams, no kids shouting, no playing football in empty parking lots, no vendors selling fruits on their wooden carts; nothing.

He walked back into the kitchen.

"Where could he have gone?" he asked.

He walked out and walked in again.

"Marc said something about a hike?" he asked.

"He didn't tell you anything?" he tried again.

"Marc said they were supposed to meet, but he didn't show up," he said.

The final time he walked into the kitchen, he said: "I'm thinking maybe I should go home in case Michael goes there, but that doesn't make sense, does it? Anyway, he has a key."

"Michael has a key to your house?" Layla asked.

She tried calling Michael again and got the same music and female voice announcing that her targeted phone number was unreachable. All the cellular networks were down as news of an imminent Israeli retaliation spread. Her father hoped Layla wouldn't hurl the phone through the window or smash a chair or kick the door. She stood up, opened the fridge and closed it. She opened the cabinet doors, one by one and slammed them shut, opened the fridge door one more time and closed it. She took her glass of bourbon and gulped it down, threw her tea in the sink, and went into her room.

"Marc said he's coming over," her father said when Layla walked back into the living room, cigarette in hand. He tried to ignore the fact that she was smoking in front of him, breaking a hitherto unspoken covenant.

"Everyone seems so preoccupied with this stupid Israeli strike," he said.

"I know," she said, "I already stopped at General Security. Stupid idiot winked at me and told me it was normal I couldn't reach my fifteen-year-old son. Said he probably didn't want to be found and sent me home. Fucking idiot."

Her father winced. He didn't like swearing.

"You should probably call the British embassy," he checked his watch. "Although I'm not sure who you'll get at this time; it's almost five."

The doorbell rang, and they both jumped. Layla stubbed out her cigarette and ran to the door, her arms wide open.

Marc ignored her look of disappointment as he walked uninvited into the living room.

"I've filled the car with petrol," he said, shaking Jeddo's hand. "They're saying we might run out if the Israelis hit."

Layla ran back to her room before Marc could ask about Michael.

When she walked back into the living room, another cigarette in hand, Marc asked her: "What do you mean he's not here? Where is he? You didn't get him from the beach?"

"He wasn't at the beach," Jeddo explained.

"Where is he then?"

"I was hoping you'd know," Layla said. "What's this little escapade the two of you were planning?"

"We weren't planning anything," he took the cigarette out of her hand and put it out. "He wanted to do this hike, something to do with Scouts, he said. He asked for my help in planning a route. He said he was doing it with a friend and that you knew about it."

"You believed a fifteen-year-old boy?"

"Yes, I believed a fifteen-year-old boy! Why wouldn't I? He called me earlier today and told me he had changed his mind. He wanted to go alone but I wouldn't let him."

"He goes hiking with you, he has keys to Baba's house. Since when did you all become so chummy with my son?"

RANA HANNA   17

Marc muttered something under his breath that she couldn't catch.

"Layla," Jeddo said. "Let him finish."

"There's nothing to finish," she said. She slumped on the couch as she tried to pluck her cigarette from the ashes.

"He was supposed to come over today at twelve. But when he didn't show up and I couldn't reach him, that's when I called you."

Layla stared ahead.

"Anyway," Marc said. "Now I'm here, so let's go."

"Go where?" Layla asked.

"Let's go find him. Let's go get our boy."

Layla

In the car, Layla's father again suggested they call the British Embassy.

"They must be able to help."

"I don't think so, Amm*," Marc said. "The embassy doesn't have time for the likes of us right now with the country on the brink of war. If the Israelis don't bomb us tonight, we have nothing to worry about; we'll wait for Michael to finish his little hike and come home. But if they do bomb, the embassy's not going to be bothering with the likes of us what with all the people they'll have to evacuate."

"Even someone like Michael?"

"Baba, what do you mean: "even someone like Michael?" She hated it when her father sounded so simple, so colonial, so old. "Who is Michael to these guys at the embassy? He's just a boy like any other, a stupid fifteen-year-old who wants to prove he's a man."

---

* Amm is a term of respect when addressing an older man.

"First of all, he's a British citizen. Secondly, he's an aristocrat. No, don't grumble like that; in some countries and for some people it still means something. Thirdly, when Adele came over some years ago, she stayed at the British Ambassador's house, so I'm pretty sure Michael will matter to them. Call Adele and tell her to call the Ambassador."

Marc nodded his head in agreement.

"I think I should call my mother-in-law just to make sure she didn't orchestrate his kidnapping in the first place to get him to England and her cherished boarding school. Wouldn't put it past her."

"Why do you say it's Adele?" her father asked.

"I found a letter in his room this morning," Layla said.

"No one kidnapped him," Marc said. "I know where he is. Hopefully he hasn't taken off yet."

"Where is he, Marc? What ideas have you been putting into his head?"

"Nothing bad," Marc winked back at her. "Don't worry."

"Fuck you!"

"Layla!" her father reprimanded from the back.

"Sorry," she said to no one in particular.

Her shoulders relaxed. Marc knew where Michael was. That's all that mattered. She was going to find her boy. She was going to get to her baby. And when she found him, she was going to hug him, and then she was going to swallow him whole and keep him safe in her womb for ever and ever.

She reached back and held her father's hand in hers.

"We're going to find him, Baba. Don't worry. Everything's going to be okay."

But her father's face was ashen. There were two other times she had seen his color drain like that: that morning when he walked into the house after three straight days at the hospital to watch over her mother, and a few months later when he dropped her off at boarding school. At the time, the color of his face was all she could see through her tears.

She let go of her father's hand.

"Can't you drive a bit faster?" she asked Marc. "There's no one else on the road."

For the rest of the way, they drove in silence on the same Jiyeh highway Layla had driven on earlier that day. On the left, shoddy, low-lying, flat-roofed buildings, obviously built without planning permission, housed car garages and bakeries and shops that were now closed, with rusting rolling shutters pulled down over the windows. The sun was setting to their right, bathing the horizon in the full spectrum of the rainbow. Layla held her breath as the dim light crowned the tops of the palm trees. It was all so peaceful. How could a country offer so much beauty and inflict so much pain at the same time? She wondered what her father was thinking, but she didn't dare ask.

Jeddo

He thought the worst day of his life had been the day he buried his wife. Then he thought it was the day he dropped Layla off in front of the sinister-looking gothic edifice that she would have to call her school. But this, this felt much worse. Michael's disappearance felt like a trident lodged at once in his guts, his heart, and his lungs.

In both the previous cases, he had gotten over his grief alone. When his wife died, he had gone through the usual rituals of burial and three-day condolences that were the norm in Lebanon. He had always been intrigued by these rituals and had once read that they had their origin in mythology. They were designed, he had read, to guide people across these difficult stages of transformation: the mind cut off from its daily life patterns and forced into a hiatus, after which the initiate would return to life, reborn, as good as new. But these condolences had done nothing of the sort for him, and as soon as they were over, he had left Layla with her aunt and spent the next three days by his wife's grave.

Those three days by his wife's grave were his condolences. He talked to her, told her how he would take great care of Layla and that she needn't worry. He reminisced with her, sang her favorite songs to her, and read passages from her favorite books. He slept by her side. His sisters were going crazy, begging him to go home. Did he forget the country was at war? He could get hit by a stray bullet. Did he forget he had a daughter? Had he given up on life? Did he wish to die? Had he lost a screw? On the last morning, he woke up smiling, bid his wife farewell and safe travels, and went home.

When he later dropped Layla off at boarding school, he returned to his wife's graveside. He knew she wasn't there, he told her, but he needed to feel a connection with her now that Layla was away. And for the first time in his adult life, he sobbed. Again, he stayed by her graveside for three days, fasting, and taking only short naps, and crying. And again, after three days, he got up and went home, his sorrow and his despair left in his dead wife's bosom, leaving him free to carry on.

But this, Michael's disappearance, this was too much to bear. He could not lose this one. The love of a grandchild was too big a burden. It was something his aging heart found too hard to cope with. He was at once grandfather, father, and sometimes mother to this child. And now it was probably because of him that Michael had disappeared. Layla turned and held his hand. He didn't dare say at that moment, just like he didn't dare say it when they were fighting a couple of days ago, that this had nothing to do with Adele. It was not Adele who was pushing Michael to go to England, it was he.

He knew Michael well; he could see himself in the boy, and so, instinctively, he knew he was safe. But at this point,

BIRDS IN THE RAIN

he would rather have concrete reassurance. Michael might be safe for now, but they had to get to him quickly before someone else realized they may have quite a prize catch lurking in their backyard.

Layla

They turned off the highway and climbed for another twenty minutes, a journey that would have normally taken over an hour. The unusually empty highway gave way to narrow, winding roads sheltered by pine forests on either side. Every few miles a barren, unfinished building would appear, testifying to the changing fate of people as the country transitioned from a war economy to a kleptocracy. They arrived to the town of Deir el Qamar just as darkness was settling, and Layla could immediately understand why the Christians and the Druzes had fought for this piece of land over centuries. Pine, olive, and oak trees nestled among stone houses with red-tiled roofs on streets that wound through the village. White and purple bougainvillea glided effortlessly over balconies.

"Your mother and I spent our honeymoon here," Layla's father told her. He pointed to an ice-cream shop across the square from the church. "She would go there every day for ice cream, to Salim's. So much war," he sighed. "God save us."

"Only the Lebanese would think of calling a place the Monastery of the Moon," Layla said. She turned to Marc, "Did you fight here?"

Marc ignored her question. They walked up a narrow street as a Muslim call to prayer began. As if in retaliation, the church bells pealed. Layla thought all they needed now was the local synagogue to call to prayer, but that had been shut down for a long time. The Lebanese Jews had crossed the border years ago.

They reached a house that opened right onto the street. Iron grilles covered the windows, from which hung brown plastic pots filled with red and pink geraniums. They knocked on the red wooden door that needed a refresher coat of paint. Layla stood, frozen in anticipation as she heard footsteps inside.

The man at the door had been handsome once, before the sun and hardship had redrawn his face. He explained that Michael had been there earlier today. He had tried to dissuade him from continuing on his hike in view of the imminent threat, but Michael had seemed adamant to continue.

"He just didn't get it," he said to Marc. "I guess we were just as dangerous at his age."

"Where did he go?" Layla interrupted, but the man simply shrugged.

"I don't know. I'm sorry," he said to Marc. "I wouldn't worry; he seemed like a determined and capable boy."

In the silence. Layla could hear only the sound of the crickets. The man's wife walked out with a tray of orange-blossom-scented lemonade. It was 7:30 p.m.

Marc

t precisely 7:30 p.m. on April 15, 1977, Marc walked into his parents' apartment in the Fassouh area of Achrafieh to the east of the capital. The electricity had been cut off again, and he followed the glow of the candle through the corridor to where he knew his mother would be. His father, he already guessed, would be on the balcony, sitting on his wicker chair, listening to the radio and smoking his pipe, despite the freshness of the weather.

"I like the smell of the orange blossoms," he would tell his sons when they urged him to come inside. They didn't want him to get hit by a stray bullet, or worse, a sniper or shrapnel from a bomb. As summer approached, he would tell them it was the jasmine and gardenia scent he was after. But tonight, Marc could smell only paraffin, anointing oil, and fear.

The war was exactly two years in, and the fighting had shown no signs of abating. Marc knew he must be stinking, having been in his military fatigues for the past five days.

He would heat some water on the gas fire and wash up. No electricity meant no hot water, but hopefully there would be cold water to heat at least.

His mother was at her station, kneeling on the floor, rosary beads in hand. On the antique wooden table in front of her stood a small marble statue of the Virgin Mary, some roses, and a white tiger lily from her balcony. She turned to him smiling as she heard his footsteps, but her expression quickly changed when she saw he was alone.

"Where's your brother?" she asked.

No further words were exchanged that evening, as his mother folded in on herself and did not pick her head up and his father sat on the balcony, smoking. Marc stood naked in the candlelit darkness of the bathroom, dipping his cloth in the tepid water and wiping himself with it. Afterwards he sat on his bed, watching the red and blue lights coming from the exchange of artillery fire in the mountains. From his father's radio, he could hear the deep voice of Fairuz, Lebanon's musical icon and most famous export, singing "Lebanon, my country, I love you."

Marc's mother died three years later, of natural causes the doctor said, but Marc knew she had died of a broken heart. She went to bed and simply did not wake up, too weak to wait for news of her missing son. Stories circulated of young men being abducted and tortured by either Israeli, Palestinian, or Syrian forces. Sometimes the family would get a notice of death, but bodies were never sent back. His mother got tired of hearing stories, he had told Layla once. Her thoughts killed her, he said. His father died three months later.

His brother never came home.

Layla

Layla stared out of her kitchen window expecting the bombs to fall any second. The Israeli warplanes had been flying low over the city all day, but now the planes moved closer, lower, slower, with intent, threatening. The Israelis had been targeting the south all day, and they would soon start destroying all means of transport and communication for the Hezbollah group (a move that would later prove futile, as more was made known about the extent of the group's underground tunneling.) She blew smoke at her reflection in the window and took another sip of her whiskey. *You should sleep*, they said. *We have to go back home*, they said. *There is nothing we can do now*, they said. *We must go home and try again tomorrow. You must sleep*, they said again. She overheard them talking in the living room next door. She did not want to sit with them. Right now, she couldn't stand them.

"Do you ever wish your brother would come back?" her father was asking Marc.

"I hope he never does."

"Why do you say that?"

"I don't want to know what he went through. I don't want to know about the atrocities he had to deal with."

"But you have no closure. How do you cope with this lack of closure?"

"I keep busy."

"These things don't go away. They catch up with you. They come back to haunt you."

"Not if you keep busy enough."

Layla did not want to sleep; she wanted to cry. But she couldn't cry. Not now. Not before she found her little boy. But the sooner she slept, the sooner she could go looking for him again. Damn him! Damn him for growing up, for having his own mind, for being so fiercely independent. Damn him for being so bright, so fearless. Damn him for being so strong. Only a few days ago, it seemed to Layla, he was nothing but a bump in her body, a flutter in her belly. It felt like only a few days ago that he was wrapped in a blanket in her lap, facing the harsh elements—the light, the noise, the stink, the aggression of the city that would become his home. How could she not have protected him? How could she not have seen it coming? How could she not have stopped it? How could she not have saved him? And how could she not have saved Sebastian?

———

"Mrs. Sebastian Cape?" the policeman had asked. He had a deep voice that matched his tall, thick stature. "I need you to come with me," he said.

The stern policeman with kind eyes explained to her that her husband had been involved in a mugging on Chicheley Street at 9:52 p.m. and had been stabbed multiple times.

"No." Layla said, "I don't think so. My husband's a pianist."

"Please, ma'am. You'll have to come with me," the police officer explained.

"I really don't think you've got the right person, officer. My husband's playing tonight at the Royal Festival Hall," Layla said. "I was supposed to go with him, but I couldn't. I wasn't feeling well. I'm pregnant, as you can see—"

"Ma'am," he interrupted her. "I need you to come down with me to the mortuary at St. Thomas's to identify your husband's body." The officer spoke in a gentle, if impatient, tone.

"Alright," Layla said after a while. "Please, just give me a minute." It was all she could say.

She closed the door and steadied herself on the wooden dining table. What did the man say? The police station? No, the hospital. The mortuary. She would go there right now and settle this matter. These idiots obviously had the wrong person, and now she had to go sort out someone else's stupid mistake. The officer had insisted he had the right person, so she would go down there and set the record straight. Then she would sue them. Sebastian would know how to sort this out. She'll call him now and ask him to meet her there.

She ignored the knocking at the door as she picked up the phone with shaking hands. What was the number of the Royal Festival Hall again? 01 . . . no, it was no longer 01, they had changed the codes recently. What was it? 0 something, 01 . . . 07 . . . she slammed the phone down. What was the number?! What was the fucking number?! Fine, she'll just go with the police officer. She looked at the clock on the kitchen wall, which read 11:11 p.m. The concert must have run late. Too many encores, as was usually the case when Sebastian played. She would leave him a note explaining to him where she had gone. Why hadn't she gone with him? She should have gone with him.

She made her way to the bathroom, holding onto the wall for support. She really hadn't felt well. The sick feeling was creeping up and lodged itself in her chest. She felt a lump in her windpipe and just barely made it to the toilet, where she threw up until bitter bile scratched her throat.

She walked unsteadily back to the piano. Sebastian had always placed pen and paper there. She put a hand under her belly, worried the baby would drop out of her womb from the sudden leaden weight on her shoulders. She picked up the pen and steadied her hand. After several efforts, she managed to squiggle:

"Don't worry. I'll be right back."

———

The day she buried Sebastian, she could only see in black and white. It was a cold day in January. The ground was white. The coffin was black with shiny lacquer like the grand piano that sat in the ballroom at Stelton Manor.

"My mother offered to give me this piano," Sebastian had told her once as he played Gershwin and she attempted to sing along, much to his distress. ("Please don't sing Gershwin," he used to say. "Please don't do that to a dead man.")

In reply to his comment Layla had cheerfully suggested they should take the offer, remove the bed, the tiny dining table, and the couch in their minuscule apartment near Victoria station and fit in the piano instead.

"We could shape a mattress like the tail, open it when we need to, and sleep in it," she had said.

"We could buy stools and use it as a dining table," Sebastian had replied.

"Yes, and we could add a shower attachment and remove the bathroom altogether."

They had agreed that, for now, the upright piano standing against the mustard yellow wall, underneath the black-and-white picture of the Exeter coach station that Layla had snapped on her first day there, would do just fine.

That first week at Exeter University, she had also met Sebastian. She had known immediately he was the one. He was bright, funny, generous, and handsome. And a musician! She knew they were kindred spirits. She loved that he was following his dreams—he could obviously afford to. She had wanted to go to acting school herself, but her father had discouraged her, deeming her way too intelligent to waste her time and talent on something that, he had said, required no skill. He hadn't saved up his money, he reminded her, to send his only child to "a vocational school." She was glad of her decision to study History at Exeter, for that is how she had met the love of her life.

She let Sebastian harass her whenever he got the chance, begging her to go out with him and complimenting her Arab beauty, her high cheekbones, green almond-shaped eyes, and naturally matte skin. "What more could an impressionable girl want?" she joked with her flatmate. They married four years later, much to the consternation of Adele, Sebastian's mother. Adele thought her only son was marrying down. A foreigner? An Arab?

"Will she come by car or by camel?" she had asked Sebastian the day of the wedding. He had let the snide question slide.

At the funeral, Layla had heard only disjointed words. *Lazarus. Jesus. Sickness. Death.* The bells of the church in Great Shelford pealed as the priest spoke. She strained her eyes in an effort to listen.

"Jesus answered, are there not twelve hours of daylight? Anyone who walks in the daytime will not stumble, for they see by this world's light. It is when a person walks at night that they stumble. For they have no light." Layla recognized the verse as John 11:9–11.

After the service when all the guests had gone, having offered their condolences that offered no consolation whatsoever, Layla stood alone facing Sebastian's gravestone. It still needed engraving. She wondered if Adele and Alastair would mention that he was a loving husband. Would they mention that he was a devoted father to an unborn baby? They had taken over all the funeral arrangements, insisting that their son be buried in the family graveyard behind the chapel at the corner of the estate in Cambridgeshire. They did not consult her, but that was fine. She had understood their need to exert even the tiniest bit of control on a situation that was spiralling into obscurity, fast.

Layla was not sure she wanted her husband to be buried in Great Shelford. She would eventually want to be buried next to him, she thought, but was unsure that she could commit, at that time, to have her remains sheltered forever in a village in Cambridgeshire she had only begun to know a few years earlier. But where else would they bury him? London? Was that fair? Could she commit to stay and die in London herself? What did she have in London now that Sebastian was gone? As much as she loved the city with all her heart, she was Lebanese. London was still a place in which she had no early childhood memories, no family pictures. She did have pictures in Beirut. On her grandmother's balcony in front of sprawling shrubs of gardenia and Arabian jasmine, on the beach with palm and olive trees in the background.

At the offices of Richards and Geroux on Chancery Lane two weeks later, Adele's heartbreak had seemed equalled only by her vexation that the Arab would inherit. Since Sebastian had not yet drafted a will, they would have to adhere to the laws governing intestate succession the lawyer had explained. Layla would be entitled to any cash savings Sebastian had, which in this case amounted to around

£50,000 and the flat in Victoria. In addition, she would receive a monthly stipend of £5,000 once the baby was born plus an education stipend once he started school. The monthly income would be adjusted annually to the rate of inflation and would be cancelled should Layla Kazen decide to remarry. A trust fund would be set up for the baby. She would have no future claim to any part of the family estate that would eventually be transferred to Lord Cape, her unborn son. The offices of Richards and Geroux would act as executors of the will, and did she have any questions?

She wanted to tell them that since Sebastian had died, she had nothing but questions. Instead, she said all was clear. She thanked the solicitor for his time and Alastair and Adele for their generosity and made her way out.

Despite the teeth-chattering cold, she had decided to walk back to their flat in Victoria. There were the odd moments when she would forget, briefly, that her life had been upended. Then in the middle of a conversation with a colleague or simply walking to the bus, she would remember that Sebastian was gone, and the force of the blow would hit her like a gale wind.

She walked down towards the river and turned onto the Strand. She was in no hurry to get to an empty flat. Later, in the evening, friends would stop by, but every day the number became fewer and fewer as they resumed their daily routines. Condolences poured in by phone and through the mail. She read the cards guiltily, feeling as if she had been prying into someone's else's business, so she stopped reading them. Her boss at work had signed her up for a meal-delivery service. He was worried about her rapid weight loss. She needed to eat for the baby, he said. But half the delivered meals remained uneaten.

Her father had come over for a few days for the funeral, but she had chased him away. She told him she wanted to be alone, that she was better alone. He had not wanted to leave her, so she became nasty, telling him he was being tiresome and overbearing, that he was crowding her. In reality, she had wanted to protect him from witnessing death again.

As Layla crossed in front of Downing Street, she thought of her father again. She wished she hadn't acted so rashly. Her father loved London. He had lived there for a while when he was a visiting post-doctoral candidate at the London School of Economics. He was what she called an Old Londoner. To him, London was the Battle of Britain, it was Winston Churchill, the embodiment of all that was great about the British, the man who'd saved Europe and the world and the best orator of all time to boot.

"Never in the field of human conflict," he often repeated to her, "was so much owed by so many to so few."

"And if you apply that to Lebanon," she would reply, "it would be 'never in the field of human conflict has so much been stolen from so many by so few,'" and laugh at her own joke.

"Be careful," he said. "Lately, things are not what they used to be, not since the war ended."

How she missed her father! And her mother! Her mother, who always had a blanket and a cup of tea ready, always with the right soothing words. How she wanted to curl up in her lap and cry. She wanted her mother to play with her hair and tell her it would be alright. When her mother had first lost her hair, Layla wanted to lop all of hers off and wrap her own head with a scarf.

"And then we could both look like that Em Salim character on TV," she would tell her mother. Layla looked at her chipped nails. Even towards the end of her life, her mother had still painted her nails red, and she always smelled of Guerlain's Shalimar.

Layla sniffed the air in St. James's Park as if in a bid to recapture the smell of her mother. Beirut always smelled of something. It smelled of coffee, of freshly baked bread, of fresh orange juice and thyme. Sometimes it smelled of trash and leaking sewage pipes, but it always smelled of something. London was green, but it smelled of nothing, only emptiness. Only cold and frost.

Layla thought of the warm January sun on the Corniche, Beirut's waterfront. She thought of long Sunday lunches at her aunt's house. She thought of the ice-cream vendor on Salim Bustros street, and how he always insisted on offering her free ice cream. She thought of how the sun set into the sea, casting its waning light onto the mountain range to the east, and swathing it in a burnt pink cover at dusk and how the houses on the mountain would slowly turn to twinkling lights in the night.

She had known at that moment, as she closed her coat around her to shield her baby from the wind, that she would go back. That despite what her father said, that despite the years of war and destruction and devastation, the news reports and the press analysis, and the negative public opinion, to her, Beirut would always be warm evenings by the sea, frangipani, and roses.

======

Layla took another sip of her drink just as the airport started getting pummeled by the bombs. Her father and Marc ran into the kitchen. The fuel depots were hit first, erupting into little fires everywhere, creating pockets of light on the otherwise black canvas outside. Michael was fine. He was safe. He had to be. She felt guilty as she remembered how she had wished she hadn't been pregnant when Sebastian had died. She had been resentful. This protruding belly of hers had stood in her way in more ways than one. She had to stay alive for it, she had to keep her sanity for it, she had to make future plans for it, when all she had wanted to do was go to the pub and drink bourbon until she could no longer see straight and smoke until she spat her lungs out.

Her father held her hand, and she rested her head on his shoulder.

John 11:9–11 echoed in her head. How had she turned from dancing in the light to stumbling in the dark?

———

When she woke up the next morning, she patted herself down. She was still fully clothed and on her bed. She wasn't sure how she had gotten there but, this wouldn't be the first time. Judging by the pain in her temples and the soreness in her throat, she must have simply passed out. Not for the first time, either.

But Layla hadn't slept. She had spent the night chasing someone. A woman. The woman was her mother. She had recognized her by her scarf. It had fallen on the floor, and she was chasing her around a house, their old house. She wanted to give it back to her, but she couldn't reach her. She wanted her mother to cover her head with the scarf so her hair could grow back. She searched for her frantically around the house. It was imperative that she give her mother the scarf back. But that didn't make sense. The woman she was chasing after had long, shiny black hair that bounced off her shoulders when she ran. So, whose scarf was it? Layla touched her own head. She was completely bald. It was hers. The scarf was hers. And naked. She was completely naked. She ran through a tall wooden door and was suddenly in another room, a big hall with endless windows that spanned the whole wall. Despite the sunlight streaming through the windows, the room was dark and dusty with damp, peeling floor-boards. This was not her home. She was in Stelton Manor. The room was empty, so why could she hear music? No, it wasn't empty, there was a piano there. A grand piano. Someone was playing the piano. Michael was playing the piano. *Michael! Michael, I found you,* she was shouting, but he couldn't hear her. She ran and ran across the room, but the more she ran the farther away he seemed to be. Then the man on the piano turned back to her. It was Sebastian.

She pulled herself out of bed. She was grateful for the smell of coffee and followed the aroma to the kitchen. Her father was making Turkish coffee on the stove. Marc was studying a map at the kitchen table. She watched as her father carefully stirred the black brew, continually lowering and raising the stainless-steel coffee pot with the long handle so the coffee did not boil over. You have to bring it to the boil three times and then leave it to settle, he had taught her. She wasn't sure if they had slept, and if they had, they didn't look it. She took the cup of coffee offered to her by her father and emptied the ashtray into the bin on the balcony.

"Did you figure out where he may have gone?" she asked Marc.

"According to Ziad yesterday, the next village he could hike to is Niha," he pointed to a spot on the bottom part of the map. "Only problem is there are several routes he could take to get there. And he could always step out onto the main road."

"And he didn't tell you which route he planned to take?"

Marc shook his head.

"Could I ask you what prompted you to believe you could help my son with this crazy plan of his without consulting me?"

"He's a big boy, Layla; he can move three inches without having to consult with his mother. But I did ask him anyway, and he said he'd already spoken to you about it."

"Really? You think so? You think it's a good idea to push my son three inches into the wilderness during a war?"

"I wasn't pushing him, Layla; I was restraining him! As if I knew there was going to be a war. The second the news of the kidnappings came out I called you!"

"Kids," Layla's father was standing at the kitchen door, car keys in hand. He looked haggard, and Layla felt the sudden urge to hug him but didn't.

"You're not going to find him by fighting," said her father.

"Where are you going?" Layla asked.

"I have to go somewhere."

"Where? Where do you have to go now of all times?"

"I have to do something."

"Now? Now you have to do something? What could be more important than finding Michael? Do we wait for you? What do we—"

"Don't wait for me. Go find your son. Anyway, it's better one of us stays here in case he comes back. You're in perfectly capable hands," he gestured to Marc. "And there's absolutely no need to worry about me." He turned his back to leave.

"When are you coming back?" Layla shouted after him.

"In three days."

She knew where he was going. She knew about his three-day rituals. Her aunt had told her about them a few years after Michael was born. Her aunt joked about how, after visiting Layla at boarding school every time, he would go "to file his report, much like our government employees here."

Layla remembered the setting exactly. She even remembered what her aunt had been wearing when she had told her that story. She remembered, because what had jarred her at the time was not the story itself but that she had somehow forgotten about boarding school. And that story opened the floodgates to memories that had long been stashed and locked away.

Mostly she remembered how strange her first night at boarding school had been. The smells had been so unfamiliar. Varnished oak, horses and cows and grass, a different brand of detergent in the toilets. That first night, as she tried to fall asleep, as she struggled to make sense of her situation, her new reality, she heard whispers. The seven other girls with whom she shared a room were intrigued. She was the only foreigner. They must've thought she was sleeping.

Where is she from?

Lebanon, she said, I think?

What the fuck is that?

Layla wondered what the word *fuck* meant.

How should I know?

Isn't that the place on the telly with the war?

Have you seen how beautiful and thick her hair is? I wish I had hair like that. She's very quiet, though.

Babs, can you fucking shut up please? I'm fucking trying to sleep.

Oh, fuck off!

The next morning the dining hall had smelled of sweet sausages and soggy toast. And tea. Not the sweet, strong tea she was accustomed to, but a bitter, bergamot-scented tea she had not tasted before. There were no olives or tomatoes or cucumbers or mint at the breakfast table, just butter and jam and cereal flakes. For the first few weeks she picked at her food, unused to the mixture of ingredients that made for fatty, mass-produced, heavily processed food that was the school lunch and dinner. Her mother had been a great cook.

As with any loss, it was a few days before Layla understood her predicament and the tears started flowing onto her pillow. In class, she understood much of the lesson, but she was nowhere near the brilliant student she had been at home. The English spoken here was different, more complicated, faster. She struggled to keep up. She kept quiet, afraid of asking questions and coming across as stupid. She didn't want to embarrass herself again. Like the other day when one of the girls told a joke. Layla didn't get it, mostly because she had no idea what *cunt* meant, nor was her sexual knowledge enough for her to understand the innuendo. But she laughed because all the other girls did. *Did you understand, Layla?* She wasn't sure if the girl was asking out of general curiosity and concern or if she was trying to snoop her out.

Yes, Layla had said, of course I get it.

Well, what does it mean then?

So she stopped congregating with the other girls. Instead, she buried herself in books, but none of the books available in the library could help her with her sex education or with the words she was not getting.

At half-term her father came especially from Beirut to spend a week with her in a nearby village. All the other girls she was trying to befriend had gone home for the week. She hated the English countryside, she told him. She hated the smell of manure. She hated lacrosse, and English food was tasteless. She missed lemons and oranges and strawberries. She begged him to take her back home with him. She would do anything, anything, if he just took her out of that hell-hole.

You must be strong Layla. You will be fine.

When he dropped her off on the last day, he handed her a green bag with Marks & Spencer's written on it. *Here,* he said, a little embarrassed, *they asked me to get you this. No, open it when you get back to your room.*

The bag had six AA-cup-sized bras in it.

She wasn't sure when her accent had turned. One summer when she couldn't go back to Beirut because the fighting had flared up and went to her aunt's house in Chicago instead, her cousin had remarked how she now said "glausses" instead of "glasses."

By the time she got to Exeter and met Sebastian, she had shed all her tears and was well and truly an English girl. She spoke eloquently, knew what *cunt* and *fuck* meant, and understood all the jokes and innuendos. The only Arab thing about her was her olive skin tone and her thick, brown, curly hair.

Now in the car with Marc, Layla remembered how Michael's hair would turn platinum blond under the summer sun and how his big blue eyes would light up when her father brought him back from their weekends away. How he would run and jump into her arms and how she would breathe in his smell in the hope that it would lodge somewhere forever in her brain. She tried to conjure it up now but couldn't.

She gasped, and Marc reached out and held her hand in his. "We're going to find him. Don't worry," he said.

Layla tried to speak but couldn't. If she could, she would have told him that she felt like she had a brick permanently lodged in her throat. And she would probably ask the question that had been on top of her mind since the day Michael was born but that she couldn't even imagine at this point. What if something bad were to happen to him?

As if reading her thoughts, Marc said: "You'll see, he'll be more than fine. He's a capable, strong boy. You should just hold him a little bit further away from you to be able to see that. It'll be alright, you'll see." He caressed her cheek with the back of his hand.

"He's lucky to have you," Layla said.

"And I'm lucky to have him," Marc replied.

"I have so many regrets," Layla said.

"We all do."

They continued driving in silence. At that point it seemed so much easier than talking.

Layla

She never tired of watching the sea. It was a deep turquoise blue today. The sea changed color every day, something to do with the absorption of light rays. Who had told her that? Was it Adele, of all people?

Her mother-in-law had come to Beirut when Michael was around five years old.

"She's coming on a reconnaissance mission," she told her father. "To make sure Michael is living adequately and that I'm not spending his stipend on myself." Upon hearing the news, her father promptly invited Adele to dinner, and Layla was relieved to have someone share the burden of Adele's visit with her.

Layla had been very worried about Adele's trip—she hadn't seen Adele since Sebastian had died—but Michael was so excited to be finally meeting his grandmother that she felt some of his excitement rub off on her. But two minutes into the visit, while she was still at the airport, the excitement turned to dread.

"I'll be staying as a guest of the British Ambassador; he's a friend of Alastair's from his Oxford days," Adele had said, looking around as if worried a guerilla force would come out of nowhere and kidnap her. Layla almost hoped one would. She resisted the image of a staged kidnapping. What she couldn't resist, however, was offering Adele a little welcome gift: a leather-embroidered toy camel she had asked her friend Lucy to pick up for her on a recent trip to Jordan.

"Here," she said to Adele. "This is for you. I got it especially from Jordan since you won't find any here." Layla smiled and kissed her on the cheek as a peace offering. And as an afterthought she said:

"I'm very happy you're here."

"I came to see Michael," Adele had replied.

"In his natural habitat?" Layla had promised her father she would be nice, but she could not help herself.

Adele bit.

"It's not his natural habitat, Layla; it's time to think of Michael coming back to England. Alastair's already managed to arrange, with great difficulty I may add, for him to attend—"

"Adele, let me stop you there. Michael's not going anywhere, he's only five years old. A five-year old belongs with his mother, not in boarding school."

"No one's taking him away from you, Layla. Michael just needs the right education; he needs to become a man. Sebastian went when he was seven, and he turned into a fine young man."

Layla gave Adele a sideways glance.

"Michael is not Sebastian," she said. *And I am not you,* is what she omitted to say. She then thought it best to change the subject.

"You'll see, Adele; a few days in Beirut and you'll be smitten."

Adele looked around her, and Layla was grateful for the new highway that bypassed the donkeys and the chickens she had first encountered upon her own return to the country.

"I doubt that very much," Adele said.

Yet despite her best intentions, Adele found herself charmed by the city and carried away by the energy exuded by its restaurants, flower and farmer's markets, beachside fish tavernas, and even its traffic jams. By her last evening her defences had fallen, helped by the many glasses of local red wine that was famous for its strength.

They were sitting on her father's balcony with their empty glasses. They were alone. Her father was doing the washing up. He refused all help when it came to household chores.

"I will ask for help when I need it," he always said. "Sit down and enjoy the view."

Her father lived on the university campus, a prime piece of real estate right on the sea. The low-lying buildings and greenery on the campus made it stand out from the concrete jungle surrounding it.

Layla hadn't known that Adele had also grown up by the sea.

"Once you grow up next to it, it becomes very hard to give it up," Adele had said. *You have a heart!* Layla wanted to shout. But Adele had been broken. She looked twenty years older already.

"Michael does seem very happy here," she conceded "and he speaks three languages! I've yet to see a British student do that at such a young age."

Layla covered Adele's hand with hers.

"Adele," she said, "you must trust that I'm doing the best I can for Michael. There is no way I will ever, ever, willingly shortchange him in any way."

"He looks so much like Sebastian," Adele said. "Especially at this age. Here," she reached into her bag, "I got you something also."

It was a small photo album of Sebastian as a boy: in his crib reaching out for the photographer, on his tricycle with the family labrador in a rose garden, in his school uniform. Layla had seen these pictures before, but she knew that Adele's giving them to her was a sign of trust, her own peace offering.

Layla pushed the album away gently back to her mother-in-law.

"Thanks, Adele," she said. "I don't want it. I appreciate the gesture, but I'm fine."

Adele placed the album back in her bag.

"There isn't one day that passes that I don't think of him," she said.

"I know," Layla said, tapping her gently on the hand. "I know." She did not know what else to say.

=====

As Layla and Marc approached Niha, the banana trees along the road soon gave way to grapevines, apple orchards, and walnut trees. Layla opened the window to let the cool fresh air in. In the distance she could hear the sound of Israeli planes hovering low, intermingled with the singing of the birds that had come to feast on the sweetness of the young apples and grapes.

"You've never been here before I take it?" Marc asked.

"I'm really upset with myself; what a beautiful place this is. And the weather! So crisp."

"It's a relatively small village. We'll probably find him waiting at the entrance. Or at the local bakery, if he's hungry."

"Marc, what do you think I should do when I see him?"

"What do you mean? There's no *should* here, Layla. There's you and there's Michael. There's no should."

"I feel like I want to hold him forever. But part of me wants to slap him for putting me through hell," Layla said.

"This is not about you, Layla."

"Why does everyone keep saying that?"

"Maybe because it's true."

"Stop here," Layla said. "I want to walk the rest of the way."

"Sure. Suit yourself." Marc stopped at the edge of the road. "But it's just going to take you longer to get to Michael."

"I've had to look after myself since I was 12 years old!"

"You don't have to justify yourself to me."

"But you're judging me. And now you don't even want to listen," Layla said.

"I'm not judging," Marc said. "I'm just saying that maybe you should try and see this situation from his side. Find out his motivations before you slap him."

"He should know better!"

"Maybe. But he doesn't. And if he has a black eye, it's hardly going to help him see better, is it?"

"If I lose him, I will die, Marc."

"No one's losing anyone. Relax. Come. I'll buy you a *man'oushe*."

And for the first time since she had seen Sebastian in her dream that morning, Layla smiled.

The village of Niha had a public garden that doubled as the village square. It was teeming with people, mostly women and children and some elderly men who had fled the southern villages with nothing but a few belongings. The Israeli army had thrown leaflets all over the villages ordering people to evacuate and blaming Hezbollah for their displacement. Yet the people stayed until one house got blown to smithereens; then everyone fled with the little they could salvage.

Children huddled together, clutching their mothers' ankle-length dresses, their snot covering the whole lower half of their faces. Some kids played tag; others cried, their cheeks colored with dirt or dust or ash, but mostly they sat quietly and stared ahead, uncertain of what the rest of the day would hold.

The inhabitants of Niha welcomed the villagers with open arms and warm cups of tea. They distributed food and comforted the weary. The local school was being fitted to accommodate the displaced for the night, or the week, or the month; no one knew for certain. No one could predict how long this war would go on. These were the poor people, of course. Their rich counterparts had already fled via the ports of Syria to brighter and greener pastures. And those who could not travel would still move to their houses in the mountain resorts to the north of the country. Those who didn't already own houses had rented some in more peaceful areas. But Niha was still eerily close to the fighting.

Layla scouted all the faces but could not see Michael. A tall, beautiful woman caught Layla's attention. She was wearing a long black robe over a pair of jeans and loafers. Her head was covered with a red and white veil, tucked neatly at the nape of her neck. The woman had big brown eyes and full lips. She was pregnant. She had two younger children at her feet and a baby asleep in her arms.

"Jesus, what is she still having babies for?" Layla asked. "She'll be lucky in a few years if she has teeth. What ignorance."

"Come on," Marc said. "You don't mean that. You're just angry and anxious."

"How are we even going to find him in this mess?" Layla stood up on her toes to glimpse above people's heads.

"Michael!" she shouted. "Michael!"

"Layla, stop shouting! Let's go to the office of the *mukhtar*."

"Where is he, Marc? Where is he? I don't see him!"

Marc

His mother had asked him that same question three decades earlier.

"Where is he, Marc? Where is he?" she had asked, wide-eyed, surprise and dread and fear enveloping her all at once. For the past two years, they had been scouting hospitals and jails and shelters. *We saw your son there,* someone would say, and his mother would rush out looking. Or *my son was in this prison, and he saw your son there. He says he's fine and not to worry.*

"He's not here, Marc!" Sometimes she said it happily, while scouting the dead in the morgue. *My son said he fought next to your son, and he saw him fall/succumb to his injuries/get whisked away to hospital.* Variations on a theme.

For three years they had looked, and then his mother had stopped searching. She died. His father never went looking; he could not handle the disappointment. He knew better than to expect his son to ever appear alive again and the sooner he made his peace with that realization, the sooner he too would be able to go.

The day Marc's mother died, an exchange of prisoners between the Christian Phalangists and the Palestinian Liberation Organization had been announced. That morning, mothers, fathers, sons, and daughters had flocked to the Green Line that divided the city into its warring Christian and Muslim factions.

"I know it, Marc," his mother had said that day on their way out of the church, making the sign of the cross and kissing the icon of the Virgin Mary that hung at the entrance. "I know he will come home today," she said.

She had stood on tiptoe to see above the heads blocking her view. For over an hour she kept scouting for the face of her son as prisoners from both camps crossed the line into the arms of loved ones, crying, laughing, smiling. But his brother wasn't there.

That night Marc had gone out on the roof of their building, rifle in one hand and a bootlegged bottle of whiskey in the other. As he drank and shot his rifle in the air, he vowed to avenge his mother's broken heart. And four days later, after he had buried her, he and his friends set up a checkpoint. They were disguised as members of the Free Liberation Army, one of the many armed factions of the war, and had shot at the first van they saw. It had four adults and three children in it.

That night he had gone back up on the roof, had snorted some cocaine, and had turned his gun on himself. As he closed his eyes and wished the images away, he felt a gentle hand unclasping his hold on the safety catch. His father helped him up and steered him downstairs to his bed. The next day Marc burned his uniform, stashed his arms in the depot, and vowed never to hold a gun again. Three months later, he buried his father and boarded a plane to France on a one-way ticket. He was twenty-two years old.

Layla

The stray dogs were excited to see the families that had swarmed the public garden of Niha. They chased after the kids, hoping for a bite of their sandwich or a bit of play with the ball. They got neither.

A medium-sized beige and white mutt came and sniffed at Layla's feet. It sat and looked up at her with dark brown eyes and eyelashes that were so long they looked fake.

"Hey, little girl," Layla knelt down and caressed the stray behind her ears. "Bet you're hungry. Shall I try and get you some food?" Layla looked up to see where Marc had gone. She saw him walking back with two *man'oushes* in hand. Layla fed half of her hot baked dough with thyme to the dog.

Marc told her he had asked around, and no one had seen a fifteen-year-old boy fitting Michael's description. Layla placed the rest of her food on the ground, and the dog settled down to feast on it.

"Alright," she said after a while.

"Alright what?" asked Marc.

"Alright, we'll wait 'til he comes."

Marc did not comment, and she understood what he could not bring himself to say: that if Michael had been on his way here, he should have arrived by now. But there was no way she could afford to think like that. Right then, the only thing to do was to sit tight and wait. She needed a cigarette. Then she realized that she had left the house that morning without any money.

"Do you have two thousand lira?" she asked. She had to admit, at just over the equivalent of a dollar a packet, the Lebanese government still made it easy and cheap for you to kill yourself.

"Here you go," Marc answered. "I got these for you," he handed her a packet of Marlboro Lights.

She smoked two cigarettes and stood up to stretch.

"Shall we go for a walk?" Layla asked.

"How long do you want to stay here? I can't help but feel our time would be used better elsewhere," Marc said.

"I want to stay until Michael comes. He will come. I know he will, and I want to be here when he does. But now I need to stretch my legs. Come."

Marc

From his position on the pavement step, Layla towered over him. Marc could not help but admire her legs when she mentioned them. They were strong and taut, sculpted by years of running. She was one of the few people he knew who could drink alcohol and run like that. The smoking was new, of course.

"There's not a problem a bottle of wine and a cigarette cannot solve," she often told him.

He never specified to her that the problem was solved only until the effects wore off. He hated to think what she would have done if she ever got her hands on the stash of drugs so freely available during the war. She would probably solve her problems forever with those. Layla stretched her arms above her head revealing a round but tight stomach. He just wanted to bury his head in there and kiss her forever. But he knew that would never happen. Not again.

She was framing people with her hands.

"I wish I'd brought my camera," she said.

"I'll go get it," he offered. "One of us should go back and check in case Michael's gone back home. Phone lines are still crossed, so your dad wouldn't be able to reach us anyway. What do you want to do? You want to stay here? I don't think there's anywhere to stay even. Any available room has been taken, I would imagine."

"I want to stay here. I'll figure it out. You go. Don't worry about me."

"Did you eat at least?"

"I'm not hungry."

"Alright," he said after a while. "I'll go and come back. What else shall I bring you?"

"A bottle of Glenfiddich."

———

Of all the times he had been to Layla's house, Marc had rarely entered Layla's bedroom. There was that night five years ago. The other time was before that even, the night they'd met. He had often thought of that night and wondered what it would have been like to make love to her. Her breath had smelled of a mixture of beer and whiskey that overpowered the flowery smell of her hair. She was beautiful even when drunk.

What had amazed him about her was her courage. She was not like other Lebanese women. She had not waited for him to approach her, beckoning him with sly under-the-lashes looks and abashed smiles. She was no temptress. No, she had walked right up to him, pressed her glass to his and said: "Drink. Don't ask."

"Okay," he said. "I won't, as long as you don't either."

She had introduced herself as a woman of few complexes but a host of problems, which, of course, he could not ask about. She had moved back to the country seven or eight years ago to deal with some "personal issues." She was a freelance photographer, she said, which he understood to mean that she was unemployed. He wanted to ask her how she could afford her drink but did not want to risk losing her. Would he care to dance? No questions, right. He had also moved back a few years before. He had been living in France, where he had undertaken a few "entrepreneurial" ventures, one of which had been successful enough to allow him to move back and retire in his home country. He now did "this and that," mostly helping underprivileged people get the ear of those with enough power to pillage the country. Would she care for another drink?

Had he known she had a little boy, he would never have offered to drive her home. She was drunk, sure, but still, he would never have made the excuse that she needed to be accompanied to her house safely. Had he known she had a little boy, he would not have let her press herself hungrily onto him in the lift. He would not have parted her mouth open with his. Had he known she had a little boy, he would never have allowed her to unzip his trousers and touch him, driving him to immediate arousal. He would never have accepted her invitation to go inside.

She had not seen the little boy standing in the corridor. She had not heard him as he turned tail and ran into his room. But Marc had seen him. The boy had spotted him, and their eyes had locked for a moment before he ran. Had the boy seen this scene before?

Marc had let go of Layla suddenly, but she did not seem to notice, as her eyes started closing. He had kept her from falling and had led her to bed and undressed her, kissing her stomach before he covered her. He did not leave that night but lay down on the bed next to her. He could not bring himself to leave. The boy had touched him, and Marc wanted to be there when he woke up in the morning. Despite her boldness and brashness and her seeming fearlessness, there was something about the look in the eyes of mother and son that had touched him and made him not want to leave this little barefoot boy and this woman he had just met called Layla.

Layla

She had forgotten about the two-headed dog. She had seen it, caught in the glare of her headlight, a short while after she had moved back to Beirut. Stray dogs had been roaming the streets of the city after dark. The streets were still not lit, and the dogs could not be seen and therefore could not be culled. She had caught a bunch of them in her headlights, and they had barked as they ran amok, away from the glare. There had been talk of imported toxic waste being dumped in the sea and in landfills during the chaos—a way for local warlords to finance their fighting—but no one had wanted to believe it. The consequences would be too harsh to contemplate, so the Lebanese did what they do best and buried their heads in the sand. And while some buried their heads, some dogs were born with two.

Layla had hit the brakes hard when she saw the monster and then had willed the image out of her mind, but for three days she couldn't eat.

She remembered those days now as she walked around the village of Niha, too restless to sit. The pup trotted at her feet. She looked around at all the people who had been rendered homeless, not sure if and when they could return home. Not sure if they still had homes to return to. This had been the case so many times before, during the civil war.

After Marc left, Layla had gone to speak to the woman with the children. She was intrigued by her. She looked both old and young at the same time. Her name was Khadija, and she was twenty-four years old. Only! She and her family had been fleeing their village when their convoy was targeted by an Israeli air raid. The van in front of theirs had been blown apart, limbs and heads flying hundreds of meters. Khadija had covered her children's eyes so they wouldn't see their father's shoe on their windscreen. Her husband, a Hezbollah fighter, had been escorting them in the van in front.

Khadija reminded Layla of Florence Owens Thompson, the subject of Dorothea Lange's famous photograph Migrant Mother. This woman, like the woman in the picture, was gazing forlornly into the distance, children huddled around her. Like Florence, she had been aged by circumstance and not by time. Khadija had young children, she was pregnant, she had just lost her husband in a horrific way, yet she sat tall, shoulders back. She had not bowed under the weight of her burden. She had swallowed it, absorbed it, and spewed it out, ready for more. She wasn't defiant; she was dignified, and Layla admired her for it. This woman had not had half the education and opportunity Layla had, and yet she exuded so much grace and refinement under pressure. Perhaps, Layla thought, her desire to interact with Khadija was a selfish act. Perhaps she wanted to engage with her in the hope that some of Khadija's dignity would rub off on her.

She wondered if Khadija would ever find herself patting herself first thing in the morning to check if she was still dressed. She wondered if she would go to bars and pick up strange men and take them home. She wondered if she would ever have to look under the bed to make sure no stained underwear had been forgotten there. She wondered if she ever needed a locked cupboard for condoms, a restraint kit, and other sex toys. She wondered if she would ever need to send her kids to spend the night at their Jeddo's house.

Probably not.

She caught Marc staring at her earlier while she stretched. He was the one who wouldn't, the only one who wouldn't. She often wondered why he hadn't taken advantage of her that night all those years ago. Maybe he was the little train that couldn't, she smiled to herself. Initially, she had been angry with him, upset that he hadn't followed the script she had so carefully crafted. He had the nerve to stay the night, to invade her space, and then to ingratiate himself to her son. He had the guts to care. Even after she kicked him out, he kept on returning, day after day at the same time. He wanted nothing to do with her, he reassured her, but could he at least spend some time with the boy? She eventually relented. He seemed decent enough, and Michael could probably use a father figure who was still relatively fit and able. Did Marc really not have any interest in her? Had she put so much nastiness and distance between them that he had stopped seeing her? He must wonder what it would have been like to have sex with her. She hated herself for being so crass, but that was, in essence, what she did. She did not make love. She fucked. She couldn't call it anything else.

When Layla explained to Khadija that her son had gone missing and that she was hoping to find him in Niha, the woman cried.

"Why do you cry now for my son and you don't cry for your husband?" Layla asked.

"Because my husband died a martyr," Khadija replied. "He died for a cause and is now in heaven with the vestal virgins."

"No one deserves to die. Not for anything," Layla said.

Khadija smiled.

"My husband did. God have mercy on him because life didn't. He certainly didn't have mercy on me. Or the children."

Layla wanted to help this woman but she didn't know how. She had no money to give her, no food. She realized she was hungry herself now. What do people do when they're hungry but have no money? She thought of all the children that stand at the traffic lights in Beirut, selling chewing gum, roses, tissues. Old men with gnarled, stumped, or missing limbs selling necklaces made from gardenias or just outright asking for money in exchange for their blessing. *May God keep your child safe; do you have 500 liras? May all your wishes come true. Only 500. May you always stay beautiful. Please, I'm hungry.*

How often she had ignored them! There were simply too many of them, mutilated, homeless, desperate. On a few occasions she had seen the same children being loaded into a van at the end of a day's shift. One early morning she watched incredulously as a little girl jumped out of a van and sat in the wheelchair that had just been opened for her by one of her companions. The girl had promptly messed up her hair, dropped one foot loosely to the floor, tilted her head to one side, closed her eyes, and parted her mouth slightly. She would stay like this at least for the next five hours or so.

"Why don't you give him something?" Michael had asked her once as she ignored the child begging at her window.

"I can't feed everybody," she had replied. "I can't be held accountable for these people! It's the system that's broken. Surely, I can't be expected to fix it!" She was ranting again. She was angry at her own helplessness in facing the ineptitudes of a whole country. She had not caused these people's miseries, and yet she was expected to solve them. These people had suffered from a war she had not instigated, a war she had suffered from herself. She had been luckier, but maybe not by much.

"I'm sorry, baby. I don't mean to shout at you. You know your Jeddo always said that as long as you can change someone's life, you should help. But I can't change these people's lives. I can't change their parents who send them out on the streets to beg. I can't fix a missing limb or offer anyone a job. They've institutionalized begging in this country, and I can't fix it. But that doesn't mean I have to fall for it. I'm not falling for it. I'm not! I'm sorry, but I'm not."

"You don't have to feed everybody," Michael said, with the simple analysis of a child. "Just feed this one, today." He then took out the sandwich in his bag and gave it to the boy with the blackened cheeks and the vacant look. He also gave him his juice.

"What are you going to eat? You have two hours of football practice." Layla asked him.

"I'll eat when I get home."

Michael had been only eight or nine years old then and had already shown more humanity and compassion than she had.

She looked around for Michael now. If only thinking about someone could conjure them up in person. She sat on the floor. At least she had her cigarettes. She took one out and patted her pockets for a lighter.

"I'd trade you half of this for one of your cigarettes."

The man addressing her was in his mid-twenties. He spoke with an English accent and was the only other person in the village dressed like her, in jeans and a t-shirt, as opposed to the long flowing robes and dresses worn by the others. He was holding a chicken and potato wrap that he had still not eaten. He was offering her the sandwich.

"That would be divine," Layla said. "Deal."

The young man sat next to her on the rocks that had been used to prop up a planter and cut the sandwich in half. The dog at her feet stood to attention at the smell of the lemon and garlic that wafted from the sandwich.

"I see you've been adopted," he pointed to the dog. "I'm James, by the way."

Layla smiled. "I'm not sure if I've been adopted for my looks or my food." She introduced herself and asked James what he was doing in these parts.

"I'm a PhD student at Lancaster University, I'm working on the social and economic effects of the repeated Israeli incursions on the people of the south and their repercussion on Lebanese politics."

Layla whistled.

"Impressive," she said. "What makes you so interested in us broken people then?"

"I love this place. I love the people. I had Lebanese friends at school, and I've been coming here for years. It's like my second home. What do you do?"

"Right now, I'm waiting for my son," Layla sighed.

"And what do you do when you're not waiting for your son?" Layla inched a bit away from James and offered him a cigarette, she lit her own and passed the lighter to him.

"Nothing."

"Nothing?"

Layla paused upon hearing her answer echoed back to her by this stranger she had just met. *Nothing.* A word that was meant to convey so much emptiness and yet was the most loaded word she had heard in such a long time. She had reduced her whole life story into one word. *Nothing. I do nothing. I am nothing. I mean nothing. I have a son. And if he goes, I will have nothing.* Layla took a drag of her cigarette. She stared out into the crowd.

"I used to have a job," she forced herself to smile at the kindness of this stranger. "Now I just take pictures."

"Oh, you're a photographer."

"No. I just take pictures."

"What's the difference?"

"A photographer tells stories, builds narratives. I just juxtapose people and objects with light and shadow. I even use props and make-up to hide their essence and make them look a certain way. Make them look nice. Acceptable to a general public."

"Whoa. Maybe you should be doing the PhD," James said. "But let me ask you this. Do you like the act of taking a picture?"

Layla nodded.

"Then you're a photographer," James said.

"I don't like my subjects, or my objects, I should say. The models. Or the pancakes. They're all, how shall I say this, so . . . still." She couldn't bring herself to say "dead."

"But they still need to tell a story, don't they?" James asked. "Perhaps you should take pictures of what you do like. Come down south with me once your son comes back. I think you'll find a lot there that'll inspire you."

"Believe me, what's lacking in this country is not the inspiration; it's the motivation. It's a country that picks at you bit by bit. Plucks your feathers away one by one. Erodes your willpower. Kills you inside one cell at a time."

"Nothing can kill you if you're not willing to die. Maybe it's time for you to start taking pictures of the living."

Jeddo

I t had rained during the night on one of his camping trips with Michael when Michael was around ten years old. Jeddo had given him a pair of binoculars for his birthday, and they had spent the day bird-watching. Jeddo knew all the birds, local and migratory, even by their Latin names.

"See that?" Jeddo said. "That is a Syrian Serin, *Serinus Syriacus*. And that is a Jack Snipe, *Lymnocryptes minimus*." He explained to his grandson that Lebanon was a very important country for birds because of its geography and topography. Birds stopped here on their journeys north to south and back, and some of them would use the country as their breeding ground because the weather was so good. Unfortunately, some of them, like the European roller, Jeddo explained, had stopped breeding here, as the bird had been heavily hunted. Michael seemed upset by this news, sad for the beautiful, small, blue bird.

"Jeddo, this is so sad," he tried to stop his tears. He was saddened by the fact that the birds were so powerless against beasts with rifles who thought it was fun to search for and kill helpless living creatures.

That night it had rained hard, and he had lain awake listening to his grandson's quiet breathing against the sound of the raindrops beating down heavily on their tent. It didn't drizzle in Lebanon. It poured. The drops were big and heavy. Michael had often asked him where the birds were hiding and if they could shelter from the rain, or if the raindrops hurt their heads and soaked their feathers. Was the rain killing them and their babies? Feeling helpless, he prayed that the rain would stop. Eventually it did, and he fell asleep. The next morning, he was relieved when he could hear them all chirp again.

On the ride home, Michael again asked him: "Can the birds hide from the rain?"

"Of course!" Jeddo had answered. "They can hide in trees and bushes and stay safe until the storm passes. Don't worry about them. They, like us, are God's creatures, and so God makes sure they are perfectly equipped to deal with any difficulty that comes their way."

He hoped that Michael wouldn't catch him out and ask him why, in that case, God didn't also keep the birds safe from hunters, but, luckily, the boy didn't comment.

"Adele says that birds can't always weather the storm," Michael said. "She says that sometimes the birds die of cold or starvation, especially if they're too young or too small."

"Nonsense!" Jeddo replied. He was upset at Michael's grandmother for being so honest with a young boy. "Don't you listen to her. I mean, you should listen to her because she's your grandmother, but you don't have to take everything she tells you to heart. Anyway, cheer up. We had a great weekend, and now we're going home to your mama."

Back at his wife's grave, Jeddo still could not get out of his head what Adele had told Michael. "What is it, Aida?"

He asked his wife. "What is it about life's vicissitudes that makes people so cruel?"

He picked up his book and started reading again. Normally, he wouldn't allow something as trivial as a phone call to interrupt his reading, certainly not his reading to his wife, and the first time it rang, he ignored it. But his caller had insisted, and in view of Michael's disappearance, he decided to answer it.

"Professor?"

He recognized the voice instantly; he could never forget a voice so deep, so authoritative. This caller had been a brilliant mind, destined for great things. They had kept in touch for a few years after the young man had graduated, until their political views diverged so much it was impossible to stay civil during their discussions. When Melhem Hussain finally joined the ranks of the militia, Jeddo could only feel contempt at an education wasted for the wrong cause.

"How are you, Melhem? Long time."

"I'm good, professor. Your grandson is here. My men found him wandering in the hills behind Niha. I just wanted you to know he's safe. I will arrange for him to be driven up to Beirut first thing tomorrow morning. It's way too dangerous to drive him up now. The Israelis are targeting every vehicle that's moving out of the perimeter. Tomorrow, *inshallah*."

"Thank you, Melhem. I really appreciate it."

He closed the phone and spoke to his wife's gravestone.

"I told you they'd find him, didn't I? Oh, Aida! Now I might cry. I wish you could see him. You'd be so proud! He's such a lovely boy, handsome and courageous and beautiful like you. And he's so wise. Oh! I knew we would find him. Thank God he's safe! I must call Layla. If only I could say the same thing about Layla. She's so lost, poor thing. I would have liked us to get along a bit better, but she is such a stubborn mule! She listens to no one. No one! Okay, okay I know what you're thinking, but I wasn't that stubborn, was I? Never mind. I'm going to have to leave you, but I promise to be back, and next time I am going to bring Michael with me."

He picked up his phone again to call Layla.

Layla

The crickets had already started their evening song by the time Layla ran into her apartment in Badaro. She had managed to find a taxi driver willing to drive her back to Beirut. The dog clinging to her chest did nothing to add color to her father's ashen face. He met her at the door, his hair even whiter than that morning.

"I thought you were at the cemetery," she said.

Marc sat slumped on the couch.

"What's with the sad face?" she asked. "What is it? Has something happened to Michael? Is Michael alright? What's wrong? Why is no one answering me?"

It was the newscaster who finally spoke.

Israeli warplanes earlier targeted the house of Melhem Hussain.

Marc pointed weakly to the television set.

"Who is Melhem Hussain?" Layla asked.

"The Hezbollah commander I told you about," her father said. "The one who called me about Michael."

"Yeah, so?" Layla asked again.

"It's where Michael was being kept," Marc said, his voice barely audible.

"We don't know that for sure," Layla said. "Michael could be anywhere!"

"Melhem called me," Jeddo said. "He called to tell me that Michael was there and that he would send him up first thing tomorrow morning."

Layla could hear a hint of a crack in his voice.

"That doesn't mean anything. It doesn't mean anything!"

She was starting to feel a little dizzy.

"Layla—"

"*Habibti*—"

"Quiet! Both of you. I need to think." Layla turned towards Michael's bedroom.

She plopped down on Michael's bed. It couldn't be. Could she withstand so much suffering? Would fate really make it so that within such a short span of time she should lose both her husband and her son? No. That was impossible. She caressed Michael's pillow. The crisp white cover reminded her of the mortuary, the sheet that had covered Sebastian's body.

———

"Is that him?" the coroner had asked.

Her soul had nodded quietly. But Layla hadn't wanted it to be him. Sebastian was somewhere else; he had to be. So, she had looked for him everywhere. In their flat. On the Tube. On the street. A couple of times in the park she thought she had spotted him, cycling, running, wiping snot from a little boy's nose. That's him! Her face would light up. And then realization would hit. These random encounters, these rare glimpses of Sebastian and of what could have been, were often violent, and she would have to lie down afterwards, sideways with a pillow wedged between her knees for a few hours, sometimes for a whole day. Sometimes she would lie down on her back on purpose in the hope that the baby's weight would crush her.

Her first Christmas without Sebastian was the worst. While she had been pregnant and living in London, Layla had dreamed of the day when she would carry her baby close to her chest, keeping him snug and warm and walking with him and Sebastian through Regent Street and Winter Wonderland at Hyde Park. They would keep each other warm and take in the sights and smells and sounds of Christmas. Her favorite activity during that period had been to go to the food department at Fortnum's. It was all so decadent, but so beautiful. She would buy some Christmas blend tea, shortbread biscuits, some whiskey marmalade, and a box of dark chocolate cognac truffles for Alastair and Adele. Her father had taught her that a gift should always be either disposable, edible, or perishable. Should your host not like it, he explained, they could either dispose of it, eat it, or watch it slowly wither away guilt-free.

Stelton Manor was always beautifully decorated. Despite its size, it was delicate. There were candles, fir branches, holly, and little Scandinavian Santas that dotted the various coffee tables. Yet emotionally it was austere, just the four of them, the in-laws, Layla, and Sebastian. So calm and quiet you could hear the wine being decanted and the cutlery clanking on the plate.

At least in Beirut you couldn't really feel Christmas. It wasn't like in London, where all the streets were lit up and the shop windows vied for which had the most ostentatious display. Instead of the lights on Regent Street, it was traffic jams; instead of icy cold weather and roasted chestnuts, it was torrential rain; and instead of caroling in the streets, it was beggars at streetlights making you feel guilty you were sheltered from the wet weather.

When her mother was alive, it was always about carols and Christmas cake and driving all the way out of the city to go to the only vendor who sold natural trees. Christmas was all about family, aunts and uncles and friends and cousins all huddled around the tree for the star-placing ceremony that her mother had created just for her. After that, the buffet would open: it had turkey with western and oriental stuffing, smoked salmon, caviar inevitably brought by a friend who worked in the Gulf where they imported it from Iran. And then for dessert: candied chestnuts, meringues, and pear and chocolate tart. And music! Christmas carols around the piano and ABBA songs and finally the iconic Fayrouz as the evening wound down and hearts and stomachs were sated and eyes were closing in satisfaction.

But then the music had stopped. Her mother had died, and the war had separated all those who had once sung around the piano and the Christmas tree, each to a different place. As Layla grew up, the warmth and joy of Christmas gave way to lights and beauty and intellectual conversation about the state of affairs in the world. And then it gave way to nothing. Just a candle-lit meal with her father: catered turkey, a good bottle of wine, and then huddling with baby Michael in bed, wondering what she had done to deserve losing Christmas.

———

Now in Michael's bedroom, Layla studied the shelves on top of the bed and reached up to grab one of his toy cars. Michael was not dead! People loved bad news.

They thrived on it, especially in war. In war, bad news made your heart race faster, and the adrenaline felt good. The death of others somehow made you feel more alive.

"Layla," Marc said. She jumped. He sat down on the bed next to her. "What are you doing?" he asked.

"Do you remember how you bonded over these cars?" Layla asked him.

"Yes."

"You know, I've always wondered, I was always so nasty to you. Why did you keep coming back?"

"Layla, I think you may be in shock," he moved closer to her and touched her forehead, not really sure what he was looking for.

"No, I'm not in shock," Layla answered. "I've always wanted to know. All these times I pushed you away, you kept coming back. Why?"

"Is this really the right time to be having this conversation?"

"Did you come back for him, or for me?" Layla asked.

"Layla—"

"I want to know," Layla insisted.

"Is it really that important for you to know?"

"Yes. It is." Layla said.

"Well," Marc said. "The answer's I don't know. I don't know."

"Well, you must know," Layla said.

"I don't. There was something. Something overpowering about the two of you. I couldn't stay away. I kept thinking of Michael. That look he had. That look you both had. You both have beautiful, big eyes. When I saw him standing there in the corridor in his Star Wars pajamas, his small feet jutting out, his little toes. Standing in the corridor . . . I . . . I . . . he—"

"Hey," Layla said. "It's okay. He's going to be okay, you'll see." She put her arms around his neck and rested her head on his shoulder.

They sat in silence for a few minutes. And then, despite her best intentions, Layla found herself brushing her lip against Marc's cheek.

"I need to go," Marc whispered and peeled away.

"Where are you going?"

"I need to find him."

Marc

It was late and the streets of Beirut were empty. The Paris of the Middle East they called it. But Paris was the city of light. Beirut was the city of darkness. For sixteen years he had been back, sixteen years since the war had ended, and Beirut was still dark. He could hear the hum of private electricity generators. Maybe the government wanted to keep the people living in the dark on purpose so they couldn't see or ask questions. *Where are our sons? Where are our fathers? Where are our brothers? Why is no one looking for them?*

Maybe he should have stayed in the city of light. For 13 years he had everything he needed, until he switched on the news one evening and saw that, with just a few signatures on a thin piece of paper, the war in Lebanon was over. He had everything he needed, and then, with that signature, he didn't. He had left Beirut in a hurry, he thought. He had run away like so many others, like bugs targeted by killer spray. He had buried his parents and run away. But he hadn't buried his brother. He had to bury his brother.

He had to find him. But he already had another family in Paris. So he stayed in Paris. He stayed until his wife hooked up with someone else and kicked him out of the house, unable to handle his shifting moods. Post-traumatic stress disorder the doctor called it. She called it unhinged.

Now, Marc parked his car under his house. At least there's one good aspect to this war, he thought: now that everyone had fled to the mountains, he could find parking easily. He looked up towards his apartment and could see the lights of the television sets flickering from a few windows. He couldn't face his empty apartment and decided to take a walk towards the seafront instead. He picked up his phone and checked the time. She would probably be having dinner now.

"Allo, oui?"

She always answered as if she was in a hurry, like she had somewhere to go, and she probably did.

"Hey baby, I just wanted to hear your voice," he told her. How much he missed her. How much he missed holding her hand, lying down next to her, caressing her hair.

"Salut, Papa, tu vas bien?"

"Yes," he said. "Yes, I'm good. I miss you. How are you?"

"I'm good. Work is good. I landed a new role in a play at the Theatre Antoine. I'm very excited. You must come to see me. What is happening there?" she asked. "Are you safe?"

He wondered when she had gotten so big as to enquire about his safety. It had seemed to him like only a few weeks ago she was seven years old and he was watching her go round and round on the merry-go-round under the Eiffel Tower. He had bought her ice cream afterwards, and they had walked along the Seine.

"What are taxes, Papa?" she had asked him. She barely rose two feet off the ground, and she was asking about taxes. He wondered where he had been the last seven years.

"What do you know about taxes?" he had asked her.

"Nothing," she had said. "But Henri keeps complaining about them."

"Oh, he does, does he?" he had tried to contain his anger at the mention of his ex-wife's boyfriend, all prim and proper and . . . French.

"Tax is an amount of money levied by the government to fund its expenses," he had said between gritted teeth, and when she looked at him blankly, he said: "Here, give me your ice cream; I'll show you what I mean."

She had given him her ice cream, and he had held it up in front of his face.

"So this ice cream is your money," he had said. "And I am the government." He had then bit into it and scooped away half her dessert.

"Thatch tactches," he had said, his mouth full of choco-late ice cream.

His daughter had cried so hard that they had to promptly go back to the ice-cream shop and buy another one.

"Papa? Are you okay?" Chloe now asked.

"Yes, baby, I was just thinking how much I miss you," Marc said.

"I'm with Maman; she says hello. When are you coming to visit?"

"Soon. I'll come soon, I promise. I love you."

"Love you too, Papa," she said.

Layla

She didn't have time to pat herself down as she ran to catch the phone that hadn't been ringing only in her dream after all. She almost slipped on a puddle of pee in the corridor. She was surprised to see her father in the living room, still dressed in the same clothes as the day before. The ringing stopped.

"Why didn't you get that?" Layla asked her father.

"I did, I—"

"What if it was Michael? Or the guy who called you? What if he's not dead?"

"I answered. There's no one on the line."

"A hospital! What if Melhem Hussain is not dead? What if he's already left with Michael?"

"Layla!" her father shouted over her shrieks. "He's fine! You'll see, he's fine!"

"Good," Layla said. "He had better be, because when I find him, I will kill him myself! What are you smiling at?"

"You looked and sounded just like your mother then. She used to say that about Marwan."

"Marwan? Who's Marwan?"

"Her younger brother."

"Mama had a younger brother? Why didn't I know that?"

"She adored him. She saw the sun shine out of his butt, as we say. She was more like a mother than a sister to him. Your grandmother was quite the socialite. This was the early sixties, the glory days of this country. Anyway, when Marwan was around Michael's age, just a bit older, he fell in love with a prostitute on Mutannabi Street—that's where all the brothels were."

"I know where Mutannabi Street is."

"There was a prostitute there. A young, pretty girl who'd let the boys rub themselves on her. As you can imagine she was very popular with the young clientele. Every time your mother and I would have to go pick him up from—"

"You knew him?"

"Of course, I knew him. Every time we went to pick him up your mother would threaten to kill him as soon as she laid eyes on him. 'I'll kill him!' She would scream in the car. 'This time I'm really going to kill him!'"

"Why didn't I know that?"

"She tried desperately to dissuade him from seeing the girl. He told her they were in love and planned to elope together. Your mother offered the girl money, but she wouldn't take it." He sighed.

"What happened?"

"One day she didn't have to go pick him up anymore."

"What do you mean?" Layla asked.

"He—" Jeddo went suddenly quiet.

"He what? Baba, are you okay?"

"He was thrown in front of your grandparents' building with a bullet to his head and a rose on his chest."

"What?! When was this?"

"Before the war. Just before your mother and I got married. She was heartbroken."

"How come I never knew this?"

"You know your mother. She cannot talk of what hurts her," he looked Layla straight in the eye. "The deeper the cut, the more she clams up."

Layla held her father's gaze.

"What happened to the guy?" she asked.

"What guy?"

"The guy who killed him."

Her father shook his head.

"What do you think happened to the guy? Nothing. It's the Wild West here in this country, it's always been like this, even before the war. The guy was probably the son of some local thug or related to him. Probably paid everyone off and left. No one saw him again. Poor Marwan."

"Why didn't you leave, Baba? Why didn't you leave when Aunt Emilia or Aunt Maysoon did?"

"Leave and go where? Every time the fighting erupted, we would say 'it's the last round.' I guess I just kept on hoping. Then your mother got sick."

"And yet you sent me away."

"How many times are we going to go over this? I sent you away because I had to. I sent you away to protect you. You think it was easy for me to send you away? You think it was easy for me to lose both my wife and my daughter? You think it was easy for me to lose my life?" His voice cracked, and Layla immediately regretted her words. She ran to sit next to him. She held his head in her arms and his face to her chest. She heard the next sentence before he even uttered it.

"You think it's easy for me now not to know where Michael is?"

"Shush," she said. "Shush. We're going to find him. You'll see. Everything's going to be alright. Everything's going to be alright. I'm sorry, Baba, I'm sorry."

Despite the stifling July heat, Layla stepped out on the balcony to smoke her cigarette. The dog trotted behind her, and Layla picked her up.

"We need to potty train you, little lady, don't we? So you stop leaving these wet spots everywhere. And you need a name. What shall we call you, huh? How about Man Ray? Would you like to be called Man Ray? Or how about Dorothea? Miss D. Yes, Miss D would suit you just fine."

She held the dog close to her and the dog licked her face.

She put Miss D down and lit her cigarette. She was desperate for a glass of wine but figured it was too early, even for her.

Her father's gaze had pierced through her when he had spoken of her mother. "You know your mother," he had said. She wanted to tell him that, actually, she wasn't too sure. She wanted to confess to him that she struggled sometimes to remember her face. That she struggled to hear her voice, to feel her touch. That whenever she remembered something to do with her mother, she wrote it down, lest that too escape her. "Your mother cannot talk of what hurts her," her father had said. She knew he was controlling himself. Layla had wanted to continue his sentence for him.

"She didn't sleep around, though. She was way more dignified than that. Way more dignified than you, Layla." It stung.

She wondered how much her father knew about her nightly escapades. Could she ever tell him the whole gamut of her activities? Could she ever tell anyone?

Marc knew. He had already picked her up from Mutannabi Street. The masked ball was being hosted by the editor of a local magazine for whom she had done a few photo shoots and whose parents had owned the building there. The place was not far from where she had taken that picture of the ten-year-old with the cigarette in his mouth. The one that had hung over the piano in her and Sebastian's apartment in London. Once the domain of the notorious Bedour al-Dahwaq and other famous madams, Mutannabi Street was, by the end of the war, nothing but empty bullet-riddled shells of buildings. Empty rooms that had gone on to house wild-growing plants instead of clients.

That night Layla had worn a backless black velvet dress with thin straps and red ballerinas on her feet. She donned her long black coat and placed the fur-trimmed mask she had been sent in her bag. "That way I can guess who you are," the editor had told her as he lightly brushed his lips against her ear. She was used to men brushing their lips against her ear while they spoke to her.

Her father had been invited to an overnight conference at the Balamand University in the North, so she had waited for Michael to go to sleep before heading out. She would only be gone for an hour or so, she was more curious than anything, she told herself. This "ball" was the one thing she had not tried yet. She would go have a quick look, see how it worked, maybe pick someone up and get back home quickly.

The main hall of the gutted apartment had been completely outfitted with red carpeting and the walls covered with plaster painted to look like marble. Ceiling-high wooden doors led into different spaces. Waiters dressed in black robes and white masks carried trays of drinks of different colors, shapes, and sizes and trays of canapés, cigarettes, cigars, and pills, barbiturates Layla guessed. At the corner of the room, a DJ with her back to the crowd played a mix of songs from various movie soundtracks and current hits. People stood, chatted, ate, and drank. Layla picked up a glass of pink champagne from one of the pass-ing waiters and wandered deeper into the room.

She picked up snippets of conversation. The Lebanese beau monde spoke of only three things: money, politics, and each other.

She heard a voice she recognized and turned to see a taller man with deep-set dark brown eyes and full lips.

"I'm so glad you could make it," the voice said. She let him take her hand and lead her into the next room. It wasn't long before she felt another hand on her arm and she turned to face the masked couple who had come to sit next to her. She wondered how many of these people she would recognize eating at a restaurant or stepping out of their fancy cars. She felt a rush of blood to the head, and before she knew it, she was kissing full red lips. The night felt festive. She loved clinking glasses instead of making conversation, fucking instead of talking, kissing instead of thinking. Next thing she knew she was being carried. Her head hit a car door, then there was the glare of the sun in her eyes, and then she was being carried again.

She had woken up in her bed. She had patted herself down and she was naked. She had reached for the phone next to her bed, but it wasn't there. Her head throbbed and her body ached. Her vulva was sore and burning. She felt her stomach heave and had run straight for the bathroom but had missed the toilet bowl by one inch and had thrown up all over the bathroom floor. She had cra-dled her head in her hands and leaned on the washbasin. When she had looked in the mirror, the reflection she saw had been crying. The reflection stared back angrily at her.

"What do you want from me?" She had asked the mirror. "Why can't you leave me alone?"

"Do you even know how you got home this morning?" Layla in the mirror had said. "Do you even know what happened at that place? What were you thinking? That you'd find love? Connection? Meaning for your sorry existence?"

"Yes, as a matter of fact, I do know," Layla lied. "What do you care?"

"You are destroying me. You are destroying us."

"I am destroying you? Who do you think you are? I'm destroying you? Fuck you! Fuck you, fuck you, fuck you!" Layla had banged at her reflection in the mirror.

When she stopped, the banging sound had continued, and she realized someone was knocking at the bathroom door.

"Mama, are you okay?" It was Michael.

"I'm okay, baby. Just give me two minutes. How was your day? Are you home early?"

"Marc is here to see you."

Layla had cleaned the floor as best she could with toilet paper, flushed it, and jumped in the shower. As the water washed the filth of the previous night off her, she sobbed. Not for the first time, she vowed never to leave her house again in search of sexual gratification.

———

Now on the balcony, Layla flicked her cigarette over the railing and looked down at the dog.

"Come on, Miss D," she sighed. "Let's go inside. No point in dwelling on the past; the present is bad enough." She wondered how long she could hold off that glass of wine.

Marc

e had known where she was. He had seen the invite. It had looked innocuous enough, but he knew what really went on at these parties.

When Michael had called him that morning, he seemed so scared. His mother wasn't home, he said. He had no idea what to do.

"Is she with you?" Michael had asked.

There was such an expectant tone in the boy's voice that he didn't have the heart to tell him his mother was in a much darker place, though he was tempted to if only to spite her. He was angry at her. One of the things that had initially endeared her to him was the gentleness with which she treated her son. How could she be so caring and so irresponsible at the same time? But, in truth, he was frightened himself. These parties were mostly harmless, a hedonistic merriment involving alcohol, drugs, and sex, but who was he to judge? But the fact that she hadn't gone home worried him, and he had tried his best not to convey his anxiety to the boy.

"Yes, she's here," he told Michael. "I'll bring her home soon."

The deserted party scene was an assault on the senses. The first thing he had noted was the stench: the oppressive staleness of smoke, the acidity of vomit, and the muskiness of bodily fluids all invaded his nostrils. Used condoms had been strewn all over the place, along with cigar and cigarette butts, martini and wine glasses, food, confetti, masks. There were still a few bodies lying around too, and he had to step over a couple before he could reach her lying on a black leather couch in one of the rooms that gave off from the central foyer. She was wearing only red ballerinas. He wrapped her up in a thin sheet he found lying around.

"Heeyyy," she slurred, as he picked her up. "What're you doing here? Come for the party?"

He took her home, dumped her in bed, and left. He vowed never to come back as he threw the sheet in a bin on the street.

But at three that afternoon, when he knew Michael would be getting home, he got antsy, and despite all he had promised himself, he found himself making his way over, convincing himself that he was only going to check on Michael.

It was when he saw her looking so gaunt and pale in her bathrobe that he lost his resolve.

"Why do you do this?" he asked her after Michael had gone to his room.

"Why do I do what?" She distracted herself from her shame by taking a sip of her coffee. She was raw, and if she showed it, Marc might take advantage of her. She could not handle truth now.

"Why do you hurt yourself like this?"

"I don't hurt myself. I'm perfectly fine, thank you." She took another sip.

BIRDS IN THE RAIN

"I hope you know you don't have to act around me," he said.

"I'd much rather you don't patronize me," she answered.

"I'm not patronizing you," Marc took a deep breath. "I care about you. God knows why, but I do."

"Please don't. And thank you for bringing me home by the way." She examined her nails. She could not look him in the eye.

"Layla, look at me," Marc said. "Look at me."

Her eyes seemed wider, darker than usual. He spoke more slowly.

"If you don't stop your destructive behavior now, you're not only going to destroy yourself, you're going to destroy your relationship with your son."

Layla looked at him. She matched his tone and his cadence.

"Don't you ever, ever tell me how to behave around my son again," she hissed.

"Layla, please, listen to me."

"Keep your opinions to yourself, Marc. Who do you think you are to judge me?"

I am someone who has been there, he wanted to say. *I understand this particular darkness. I am someone who knows this level of pain and anger. I know that sometimes the only way to relieve pain in one place is to hurt yourself in another.*

"No one," he said. "I am nobody. I am not judging. I'm just trying to help. Why do you do this, Layla? What do you want?"

"I want you to get out of my house."

"Layla, please listen. Don't lose it now. I'm only thinking of Michael," Marc said.

"Get. The fuck out. Of my house."

"Fine," Marc said. "I'll leave. But next time you're out on one of your escapades and you pass out at a party or an orgy of yours, please tell your son not to call me." He got up to leave.

"What's that supposed to mean?"

"You're bright enough, you figure it out." What was it about this woman that left him so unbalanced?

"Oh, really? You think so? Well, at least my escapades don't get people killed!" she had screamed to his back. He turned just in time to see her look of sorrow and shame, and he knew he had pushed her too far. He had tipped her over. He was angry with himself now. What was he trying to do? What was he trying to achieve? Why was he always trying to help her? His therapist had once told him that nobody could help him. He had to learn to help himself. But he had had an anchor. He had a caring wife and a loving child, and perhaps most importantly, he was in France, far away from Lebanon, far away from the source, the trigger. Ever since he had met Layla, he had been trying to help her find that anchor, something to hold on to until the light shone through. Maybe, perhaps, that anchor could even be him. But in the deep, murky waters that surrounded Layla, there was no anchor to be found. She did not even seem to know where she should start looking.

He had left her house and driven straight to his boxing gym.

"Find me someone to spar with," he told the coach. "The stronger the better."

Michael

When I was about eleven years old, our neighbor downstairs, Mrs. Kamel, lost her cat and cried for days.

"I can't help it," Mrs. Kamel had told my mother. "I know she was old. Everybody thinks I'm crazy to cry so much over an old, dead cat, but she was my cat, you know what I mean?"

"I know exactly what you mean," my mother had replied. She gave our neighbor a quick hug and patted her on the shoulder. "Call me if you need anything. Or if you just need to talk."

I liked our neighbor. She would often give me lollipops when she found me waiting for the bus at the foot of our building early in the morning. Of all the neighbors in our building, she was the only one who never asked after my mother. The others would suggest that maybe she should be waiting for the bus with me, but frankly I didn't see the point. Neither did she.

"Why should we both get up so early in the morning?" she would say. "Only one of us is going to school."

I could see her point. She often stayed up quite late. I think the neighbors were just being nasty and nosy.

"Gossip," my mother would say. "The Lebanese were born for it. They probably even invented it."

But not Mrs. Kamel. She never said anything like that. She never gossiped. She just asked me if I wanted a lollipop and went on her way. Sometimes, she rubbed my hair.

At dinner that evening, I asked my mother why Mrs. Kamel was crying so hard over a stupid cat.

"First," she said, as she dipped her fork into my gnocchi, "you don't know if the cat was stupid. Second, it's not the cat."

I looked at her, gave her my inquisitive, could-you-elaborate-on-that look in one eye and my cold, hard, could-you-stop-eating-my-gnocchi stare in the other.

My mother sighed. "She's crying for herself," she said. "She's sad, she's old, and she's alone. She's probably missing her husband, or mother, or daughter, or anyone else she's been grieving about silently all these years. And now, through the death of her cat, she's having to miss them all over again. It's not the cat," she put her fork down. "It's never the cat."

I'd been shocked to see an adult cry, especially Mrs. Kamel. She was always so nice and smiling with her purplish hair and her kind eyes. And strong! Never accepting help from me to carry her grocery basket up the stairs when the lift wasn't working, which it often wasn't.

"Don't you dare," she would say and slap me playfully on the hand. "How else could I get my exercise?"

So, to see her crying like this had rattled me. As far as I knew adults never cried. My mother never did! Jeddo didn't, and Marc certainly didn't. Although I do remember Jeddo once telling me about my mother crying for thirteen and a half days when I was born.

BIRDS IN THE RAIN

"She was so happy to have you that she buried her head in your chest and sobbed." He had a habit of pressing his hands to my face when he spoke to me. "She wouldn't let go of you, and she wouldn't stop crying until I threatened to take you away from her because I was worried you would drink her tears."

I wanted to believe Jeddo. I did. But when my mother is happy, she dances and sings; she doesn't cry. She told me once that when she announced to my father that she was pregnant, he picked her up and hugged her and danced with her around the room. Every day after that, she told me, he would play the piano for me, despite his very busy schedule, and she would sing and dance with him. Bach, Debussy, Satie, Mozart, even Glenn Gould and Scott Joplin. Anything and everything, she said, depending on the time of day and the mood he suspected their unborn child, meaning me, would be in.

I asked her often to repeat that story. I loved it. But every time it would end there. Every time she told it, I hoped she would go a little further with it, tell me a bit more. But every time, that's where she would end her story. That's where her expression would change and she would go off to her darkroom. She spent hours in there.

Now that I think about it, maybe that's where she went to cry.

I wanted to believe Jeddo. I really did. But up until a few days ago, I could've believed that my mother never cried. Ever.

Have you ever seen your mother cry? It shakes the ground beneath your feet. If you have seen your mother cry, you'll know what I'm talking about. And if you haven't, count yourself lucky.

"You sound just like Adele," she was screaming at Jeddo. "She lost her son, and now she wants to steal mine!"

"Stop it, Layla. Stop being so melodramatic. No one wants to steal anyone's child. We only want what's best for Michael," Jeddo said.

"You stop it. 'I only want what's best for Michael.' Like you wanted the best for me? You threw me in boarding school as soon as Mama died. In another country! Look at me: I am like a dead tree. Rootless, fruitless, and bare. I don't belong here: I don't belong there. And it's all your fault! I lost my childhood and now you want Michael to lose his."

"It was the war, Layla." I edged in closer to hear him better. They hadn't heard me come in, and I wanted to stay hidden.

"It was the war, Layla. You always say the same thing. It's always the bloody war! Like the war is a good enough reason to dump me in boarding school 3,000 miles away. Uproot me from everything I knew and loved. Uproot me from my only sense of security. Do you have any idea how that felt? And now you want me to do the same thing to my son!"

"You're right. Maybe I should have left you here to turn into a drug addict like Zeina."

"Not everyone who stayed here turned into a drug addict."

"You want me to apologize for doing what was best for you? We were living in a dangerous area. Schools were opening two days a week, at best! Militiamen were walking into houses, stealing, raping. What did you want me to do? Look at what happened to your friends, to our neighbors. To Myriam and Zeina and Maya—how many examples do you want me to give? What did you want me to do? Leave you here and risk your life? Your future?"

"You call what I have now a future?"

Jeddo sighed.

"It's in your hands," he said.

It was getting cryptic.

My mother sank to the floor. Tears immediately welled up in my eyes, I wanted to turn and look away, wanted to run to my room, but I kept looking.

"I don't know," she said. "I don't know anything anymore."

"What do you mean, you don't know?" Now Jeddo was getting angry. "Of course you know. You've heard the stories. Men torn apart by jeeps driving in opposite directions, neighbors and friends killing each other, covering their faces in balaclavas so they don't recognize each other! You know of the dead, you've heard of the missing in the thousands! Marc's own brother! No, Layla, don't tell me you don't know. We all know, we just don't talk about it. And just because we don't talk about it doesn't mean it didn't happen!" He was shaking.

"I don't want to send him away," she wiped snot from her nose. "Don't make me do it please! He's just a boy."

Jeddo's tone softened.

"No one's going to make you do anything, Layla. But you need to understand that he's not just a boy. He's almost a man. He's taller than you and me put together. It's time he gets closer to his roots, to his heritage. His father is English. He is English. His grandfather is dying, and he's the only child of an only child. And he can go to a top school. What exactly did you have in mind? That he stay here and wait for the next war? The next explosion? Can I remind you what it's been like here since they killed Hariri? First the Prime Minister, then anyone whose opinion is unwelcome."

"Not now. He's too young."

"Stop shielding him. You can't protect him forever. When did you even visit his father's grave with him? You don't even have pictures of Sebastian in the house. It's almost as if he never existed. It's almost as if by denying his existence you don't have to deal with his disappearance. What does Michael even know about him?"

"I'm sorry if my husband is buried in a different country."

"Like you would have gone! You never even go to visit your mother's grave down the road. It's as if you're trying to deny people you've loved ever existed!"

My mother sobbed quietly, and I could no longer contain my tears.

Jeddo took a deep breath and continued, a bit calmer. "Please don't cry. I don't want to fight with you. You and Michael, you're all I have."

"He's just a boy," my mother said again. I really wished she would stop saying that.

"He's a growing boy," Jeddo corrected.

"I can't lose him, Baba. I can't. I think my heart will actually, physically, break," my mother said, and I wanted to run to her, to hug her, to reassure her that I wasn't going anywhere. But at the same time, I was angry; Jeddo was right. Other than the story of her pregnancy, my mother hardly ever spoke to me of my father. Most of what I knew about him came from Adele. The last couple of years I had started spending more time with my English grandparents over the summer. I pretended to know everything they told me about him because I didn't want Adele to get upset with my mother. The other day, my mother had accidentally left her cupboard drawer open, the one that's normally locked. I found a picture of my father, and I took it. I also took a cigarette. But when I saw the packet of condoms and some funny-looking dildos, I bolted.

"*Habibti*," Jeddo said. "This is not about you."

No, it wasn't. It was about me. I ran to my room, embarrassed by my own tears.

It's all true. Everything Jeddo said was true. My mother did cry.

I lay down on my bed and stared at the ceiling. I didn't know what to do, but I knew I had to do something. I wasn't just a boy. Everyone seemed to see that except her. I had to prove it to her. I had to prove to her that I could take care of myself so she would stop worrying about me, so she would stop crying maybe. I slid into the bathroom so no one could hear me, and I called Marc.

Michael

The guy Marc and I were supposed to go see first, Ziad, tried to dissuade me from going on my hike. The situation looked uncertain, he said; I should go back home. I assured him that I had Marc's blessing. Marc couldn't make it, I lied, not wanting to go into detail as to why I never went to our meeting point. I wanted to get the maps and get moving, to get as much of a head start as I could before Marc realized I had skipped on him.

When I'd called him this morning to tell him I wanted to do the hike alone, he wouldn't let me. He was just as bad as my mother. I had to pretend to agree to let him come with me just so he would lay off me. We agreed on a meeting point. I assured him that I had my mother's permission. Then he mentioned that we would come here to Ziad's as a first stop to get the maps of the hiking trails. His friend Ziad had worked with this American association that was helping restore the trails north to south.

Ziad finally relented and gave me the maps. Was I sure of what I was doing? I assured him that I was and that I knew these trails well. He also gave me a charger for my phone. I didn't have the heart to tell him it was the wrong one, so I kept it. But then I gave it back in case it was his only one.

"I'll be back in three days," I said. I didn't think my battery would die, I said, but he insisted and offered me some lemonade. He gave me some dates and fresh almonds for the road and wished me luck. He gave me his number and told me to call him in case I needed anything.

I knew these trails well, I told Ziad. That bit was true. I'd hiked them before with Jeddo. When I was younger, around six or seven years old, my mother often sent me to sleep at his house on weekends. At first, I cried at night. I would imagine her arms around me, burying her face in my neck and covering me with kisses. I would imagine her laughing face as she made me fly high over her, hoisting me up with her feet and flopping me back on the bed. I would cry. I would then walk to Jeddo's room and poke him awake and ask him to take me back home in the middle of the night.

"I want to see my mommy," I'd cry. "I want to eat ice cream with mommy."

After a while, Jeddo got the brilliant idea of taking me camping on weekends when the weather permitted. (His other brilliant idea was to stock his freezer with ice cream for when it didn't.)

"We're going on an adventure," he would say. "We're going to hide in the forest and see if your mother can find us." I used to love these long games of hide and seek, and it took me a while to understand how come we always won.

One evening around the fire, he told me how he used to hike these same trails with his own father but that he never got the chance to do that with my mother because of the war and because he had to send her to boarding school, but that he would often come out here alone. I asked him if he was ever afraid to hike with all the militiamen lurking around in the wilderness. We learned nothing about the war in school, but Marc and I talked a lot about it, and he gave me some books to read.

"You can never be afraid of your own country," Jeddo declared.

"Marc says bad things happened here," I said.

"Bad things happen everywhere," he replied. "You can be afraid of people, but this," he had taken a handful of soil from the ground, "you can never be afraid of this. You can never be afraid of the earth, the sky, the stars, the trees. Look at these trees. Listen. Listen to the birds. Did you know that in folklore a bird is the symbol of the soul? Birds are like guardian angels keeping us safe. They are a sign of life, a testament to the miracle of living, not fear."

I really needed to remember Jeddo's reassuring words now. I sat down on a tree stump and took some soil in my hand. It felt dry and loose, not cool and calming like it had felt that time with Jeddo. It was getting dark, and I had been walking all day. I was a little afraid, I admit. But then I remembered that this was my country. I couldn't be afraid of my own country. Even if my father was English, even if I wasn't born here, I've been living here since I was just a few months old. I grew up here, I go to school here, I speak Arabic. I have friends here. I support Lebanese basketball teams. Maybe I didn't have a Lebanese passport on account of my father being English, but I'm as Lebanese as the next guy, whether the guy at passport control likes it or not.

———

The sky was clear, and the air was clean, and I had obviously not veered too far inland so from where I was, I could see the lights of the coastal cities twinkling in the dark far away. I guessed the bigger cluster of lights was Beirut. I felt like some kind of bird god perched above and pretended to be watching over my mother and Jeddo and Marc. I felt like an eagle soaring in the sky above them. But, naively, I also hoped that should anything happen they would see me. I decided to set up my tent for the night. I wondered if Jeddo would be proud of me.

―――――

I woke up to find Beirut burning. Lazy smoke billowed out of buildings. Standing there on the mountain overlooking the city, I felt like a character in an apocalypse movie, someone who'd woken up to find his whole world invaded by aliens shooting at Earth. Whenever we watched these kinds of movies, Jeddo would tell me that in fact the aliens were only shooting at America, because Americans saw themselves as the whole world. But that couldn't be true because here they were shooting at us, not the Americans. How could I not have heard anything? My mother told me that, as a child, she often slept through bombing raids and was woken up in the middle of the night to huddle in the central staircase where there were no windows that could shatter over their heads. Or, if it was really bad, they would go down into the basement of the building between the foundation columns. She seemed to speak so casually about something so terrifying that I didn't believe her. And yet I had just slept through what must have been a whole night of bombing. I had slept through the apocalypse!

I couldn't fold my tent fast enough. In my hurry I wasn't letting the air out properly and it kept on reopening. I couldn't just stay put. I had to go, I had to get out of this place. I had to go home. I flipped my phone open to call and realized it was dead.

What was I going to do now? Maybe my mother was right; maybe I was just a boy. What had possessed me to do this? Why hadn't I waited for Marc or asked Alexander to go with me? Someone; just not on my own. Alright. Alright. Breathe. This was my country. Breathe. This was my country. Calm down. There wasn't much point in flipping out. As Jeddo says, flipping out will get you nowhere, and I needed to get somewhere, now! My best option was to keep moving, to go to my next stop, which was the village of Niha. It was quicker to go to Niha than to retrace my steps. Breathe. Once I get to the next stop I will figure out what to do. At least they would have a phone there or a charger, and I could call Mama.

Calmed by my little pep talk, I packed my sleeping bag and my tent properly and started walking again.

Michael

O nly after hours of walking among pine trees and reaching nowhere did I wonder if I was lost. I reached into my bag for the maps, but they must have fallen out while I folded my tent.

I heard footsteps. I was relieved to see three guys walking towards me. But my relief quickly faded when I saw that they were carrying weapons. I couldn't tell the model, but one thing I knew was that these were not hunting rifles. The boys did not look much older than me, and they looked haggard. I must've looked haggard to them, too. Their eyes were bloodshot. They were all wearing a uniform of sorts, dark green cargo pants and black t-shirts and Doc Marten-style boots.

I couldn't place them. Friendly? Unfriendly? They were courteous but with weapons on their backs, I wasn't sure what to think.

"Where are you from?" the one with the unibrow said.

"Beirut," I said.

"Where in Beirut?" he asked. I knew he was trying to place me. In such a socially divided country, your name and your location were almost like a DNA test in terms of what they said about you.

"Badaro," I said. One of the few areas still religiously and socially mixed.

"You live in Badaro," said the second one. He had small, close-set eyes that made him look quite menacing. He stood with his face very close to mine, and I had to admit that I was intimidated.

"Where are you originally from, blond boy?"

"I'm from Beirut," I said. His teeth looked like they hadn't been brushed in weeks. His breath reeked of organic decaying matter.

"What's your name, blondie?"

"Michael."

"Micol? Micol what? Do you have papers on you, Micol?"

"No. I don't. Michael Cape," I said.

"Cabe?"

"Cape," I corrected him. He winced and adjusted his gun on his shoulder.

"Cabe," he insisted. "What's your father's name?"

"Marc," I said. I was obviously some kind of anomaly to them. A blond, obviously foreign-looking boy who spoke with a perfect Lebanese accent. "Marc Cabe. Marc Kazen." I was starting to get flustered.

"Decide," said the third one as he flicked his cigarette into the dry shrubs. "Cabe or Kazen?"

"You can start fires like that," I said to him, to which he promptly put the butt of his gun under my chin and stood so close to me our lips where almost touching. The stale smell of nicotine on his breath made my stomach turn.

"My name is Michael Cape Kazen," I said through gritted teeth. I hefted my backpack and stood up taller, a trick that Jeddo had taught me. Don't ever cower, he always said, especially when you're afraid. Don't be a dog; be a crab. When you feel threatened, don't cower: stand up taller.

"Cape is my middle name," I hissed.

The man in the middle, who I assumed to be the leader of the group, eyed me with amusement. He unseated his rifle, pointed it towards me and slid my backpack off with it. I fought back my tears. My mother had mentioned how difficult it had been when she first moved back and was trying to get her stuff from the port, not knowing who was corrupt and who wasn't. It was impossible, she said, to decipher who was trying to extort her and who was genuinely trying to help her. The war had ended just a couple of years earlier, and it was difficult to tell who wanted to rebuild and who benefited more from a state of chaos. Ten years later, she could understand the language and the mannerisms perfectly, she said, but it had taken her many years, many tears, and a lot of frustration.

The leader of the gang smiled at me. He picked up my bag and started rummaging through it.

"What are you doing round these parts alone, Micol?" he asked.

"Hiking," I said.

"Hiking? Alone? How old are you?"

"Sixteen. Next month."

"Why do you have a pair of binoculars in your bag, Micol?"

"I like to look at birds."

"Birds?"

"Birds."

"You'd better come with us," he said.

The three musketeers, as I'd started to think of them, did not blindfold me. They did not handcuff me. And they didn't talk to me either, which scared me the most. They simply asked me to go with them, and I knew better than to argue.

These guys looked a lot like Marc would've looked thirty years ago, I imagined, and I wouldn't have messed with him then. I felt guilty for using my mother's name and Marc's, but I really needed to come across as Lebanese as possible. I couldn't place these guys, and I wasn't sure coming across as a foreigner with a foreign name who spoke Arabic was a good idea.

I didn't dare ask where we were going. The less I engaged with these people, the better. I needed to get to someone's office, speak with someone in a senior position. That's what I'd learned from my mother. In this country, don't mess with the middleman, go straight to the top. The people at the top are the only ones who can actually do anything. Don't bother with anyone else.

——————

I remembered a time at the airport when my mother offered me to the passport-control guy. We were traveling together, to Greece I think, and the guy at the booth had said I couldn't leave. (My mother later explained to me that it was because my residency permit had expired two weeks before.) That's when she suggested he could keep me. I almost shat my pants.

The officer looked at her in amazement, and then she launched into her rant. My mother speaks quickly when she's angry, so I only caught some words like "shame on you" and "ridiculous" and "Lebanese" and "mother" and "passport." "I am his mother!" I remember her screaming. "And if *I* am Lebanese, then *he* is Lebanese."

We ended up in someone's office. We always ended up in someone's office. But that person was nicer, and he let us through. The man in the office always let us through. Maybe because my mother spoke to them more nicely. Jeddo told me that when she first moved back to Lebanon, she always used to get into trouble at checkpoints, asking the Syrian army officers if it wasn't time they returned home and left the Lebanese alone.

"Your mother has a problem with men in uniform," he said. "If they're wearing one, she feels compelled to scream at them. *Contumacious.* Yes, that's the word."

I remember being so impressed with that word that I wrote it down on my hand and looked it up in the dictionary as soon as I got home. I wanted to memorize it so that I could impress Adele with it. Adele loved big words.

"I'm surprised no one's beaten her up yet, or thrown her in jail," Jeddo continued.

"Maybe one day," I offered. "Has she always been," I looked inside my hand "con-tu-ma-cious?"

Jeddo laughed, but only for a while. He got sad again, kind of like my mother when she told me the story about her and my dad.

"No," he said. "She's always resisted authority, but before your father died she never used to scream."

I'd wanted to tell him that sometimes I heard her scream at night, but somehow I thought he knew that already. I wondered if he knew about the other noises, the moans and the giggles I'd hear sometimes when she thought I was tucked away and asleep in bed.

———

By the sound of it, we seemed to be walking straight into the bombing. The noise of the low-flying fighting planes was getting louder, masking the sounds from my own growling stomach. My captors seemed oblivious to the noise, but I jumped at every explosion. I could almost hear the rocks and earth burst and fly through the air. I was very scared, but I couldn't show weakness in front of these guys. God knows how they would react.

After walking for a couple of hours, we left the path and walked towards a house that stood lonely on a hillside. The sun was already low on the horizon, and lights from houses began to dot the countryside. I could tell the house we were walking toward was newly built because the traditional stone used in the villages was still so white and the red brick hadn't yet faded. Some chickens roamed freely in the front garden that had only been half planted with geraniums and olive trees. A swing swayed lightly, as if had just been vacated to announce our arrival. It was dinnertime, and I could smell fried potatoes and lemon, and I almost fainted from hunger.

The door to the house was open and led into a darkened room with old ceramic tiles in the most beautiful colors. A mantlepiece to the right of the room carried pictures of young men who looked around the age of my captors. The pictures had green frames and black sashes across the bottom left corner. Arabic calligraphy spelling *martyr* was written on top. A short, stocky woman with an apron, who I understood to be the housekeeper, came out from the kitchen and pointed to the room across from the hallway. She looked me up and down, and I couldn't make out what she was thinking.

"He's in there," she said. "Go in."

The man sitting in the armchair watching TV was bald, with wide, square shoulders. He was a big guy. He had a tumbler of whiskey on the table in front of him. For the first time since I woke up this morning, I understood that things were not good. The TV presenter was wearing an armored vest and jumped every few minutes when a whizzing noise would startle her. Black smoke billowed behind her. The country was definitely at war.

Without turning back, the man in the armchair motioned for us to approach.

"What have you guys picked up now?" he asked, as he looked me up and down much as the woman had. But he could not hide the faintest of smiles, and I could tell he was amused by what he saw. I wondered if that was a good thing.

"Sir, we found him walking in the woods behind Niha."

"Walking in the woods behind Niha. Alone? How old are you, son?" He looked a lot like my math teacher, and I couldn't help liking him.

"I'm almost sixteen. Sir."

"Where are you from?"

"He didn't have papers on him, sir," interjected the leader of the group. "And he had a pair of binoculars in his bag."

The man I have come to know as Sir ignored him. He looked at me and expected an answer.

"I am Lebanese, sir; I live with my mother in Beirut."

"And your father?"

"He's dead, sir."

"*Allah yerhamo* (may God have mercy on him)."

He continued to stare at me. He looked kind, but I was thinking maybe I shouldn't like him so much because I really couldn't tell what he was thinking.

"Do you know why you're here?"

I had no idea.

"No, sir."

"These guys think you're a spy."

Holy shit! Sir watched me closely, I think he wanted to gauge my reaction, which was nothing less than shocked.

"Well," he said. "Are you?"

He heaved himself off his seat, and for the first time I could see just how big he was. At almost five feet, eleven inches, I wasn't short myself, and Sir towered over me. He put his large hand on my shoulder.

"Am I what, sir?"

"Are you a spy?"

"N . . . no, sir . . . I'm only fifteen!"

Sir cracked up laughing.

"Did you tell that to these assholes here?" He pointed to my captors.

How was I supposed to answer that?

"What were you doing out in the woods by yourself?"

"I was hiking."

"Hiking? Alone? During a war?"

"There wasn't a war when I left the house." And again he roared with laughter. I seemed to be amusing him. Too bad I was about to pee my pants.

"And why were you alone? Don't you see it's dangerous in these parts? Where were you going to?"

"Just to Niha, sir. It was just a hike I was doing for my Scouts group. I just—I swear I'm not a spy. I got lost and—" And I started crying, like a lousy baby.

"Why are you crying? You scared? Who's your father?"

"My father's dead," I said, not sure if I was crying for fear or for my dead father.

"Yes, I heard you the first time. What was his name, I mean?"

"Sebastian Cape."

"You're a foreigner?"

"No, sir! My mother is Lebanese."

"But your father isn't. What's your mother's name?"

"Layla Kazen."

"Kazen?" The name seemed to make him think. "What relation are you to Professor Nadim Kazen?"

"He's my grandfather." A flutter of hope went through me, and my tears stopped flowing immediately.

Sir smiled.

"I know your grandfather. I took a course with him at the university. I really liked him. Very knowledgeable man. Is he still teaching?"

"Sometimes," I said.

"Son, why don't you go into the kitchen and get some food? You look like you could use some."

"I need to call my mother," I said.

"I will contact your Jeddo and tell him you're safe and that we will drive you up tomorrow at first light."

"Do you know his number?"

"I know everything." He patted me on the shoulder and gently turned me around towards the door.

I sat at the plastic table in the kitchen on a rickety wooden chair and devoured tabbouleh and fried potatoes that, it turns out, were actually being prepared for me. I overheard Sir screaming his head off at the goons who had captured me and brought me here. Maybe he left the door open on purpose so I could hear.

"Fucking idiots, couldn't you see he's just a boy!"

They mumbled answers that I couldn't catch.

"Binoculars? Are you a total idiot, or do you just behave that way? Do you think every foreigner is a spy? What would a fifteen-year-old know?"

I'm pretty sure I heard a slapping noise that made me perk up like a dog that's just smelled a sausage, but the woman who'd given me my food and who now stood at the sink didn't seem to budge, and I thought maybe I'd misheard. I hoped so. Not that I didn't like the idea of the chief goon getting slapped, but I really wasn't up to any violence right now. Besides, I didn't want him taking it out on me later.

I wanted to call my mother. It sickened me to think that she would be so worried about me. But Sir said he would call Jeddo, and something told me I could not push or challenge this man. This was obviously a guy who was used to giving orders and not being on the receiving end.

I finished my food in silence, listening to the chickens clucking outside. I had no idea whether I could trust this man. Judging by the number of guns I could see strewn around so casually, I figured I probably shouldn't.

———

My mother always told me that if I had a problem that seemed too big to deal with, I should just cut it up into smaller pieces and deal with one piece at a time.

"Just like a piece of kibbe," she said. Kibbe was one of my favourite dishes, a sort of meat pie cut into small lozenges. There was this big piece of kibbe on my plate with yogurt, and I was complaining that it was too big to eat. She told me to cut it into smaller pieces and to eat as much as I could handle.

"See where you get to," she said.

When I'd finished my plate, she said: "See? No problem is too big when you cut it up into smaller pieces." And with that she lunged at me and pretended like she wanted to eat me, and I remember how the tickly feeling on my neck felt so good. I'd wanted to ask her after that time why she couldn't seem to cut her own problems into smaller pieces and gobble them up. But I didn't dare. I didn't know if that would make her angry. My mother was no fun when she was angry. I had seen her angry at Marc before, the first time I met him. I woke up one morning and found him in our kitchen. He looked nice, not the scary and wild-eyed man I had seen the night before. I had frozen in place then, not sure whether he was attacking my mother or kissing her. I had been so scared I ran to my room and locked the door and sat in bed waiting. But the truth is I'd seen other men do that to my mother, and she seemed just fine the next morning, so after a while I fell asleep again.

But the next morning, he was still there, which was odd. He was drinking coffee and staring out the window, as if waiting for me to wake up. He smiled at me and held out his hand to shake, and he had seemed real.

"Hello, young man," he said. "I'm Marc. What's your name?"

I didn't answer, but I did run to my room to get my collection of toy cars. If this guy was real, if he was *bona fide*, then he would want to play with my cars.

But when my mother found us racing cars on the kitchen table, she had gotten a bit upset and asked him to leave. Marc had stayed calm, even though my mother hurled words I couldn't quite understand at the time. I cried when he left, and when my mother saw me crying, she knelt beside me, hugged me, and said she was sorry and that this would never, ever happen again.

She had lied, though. Sort of. I did see other men come to our house, not as many as before, but I never saw them again in the morning. They seemed to vanish during the night. But Marc did come back. I don't know how, and I don't know why. My mother called me from my room one day and said that Marc would like for the two of us to play with my cars if I wanted, and I ran to my room and got my brand-new Hot Wheel set to show him.

———

So, my problem was this: in the hope of going home the next morning, I could stay in a house loaded with guns from floor to ceiling and risk being attacked by a guy whose feathers I'd ruffled, or I could leave and try to find my own way back home. I tried to break up the problem into smaller pieces, looking at the pros and cons. If I stayed, I would go home the next day, but most probably I wouldn't survive the night. I really did not like the way that guy had looked at me, his eyes narrowly slit and his thin lips forming a malicious smile. I could leave and try to find my own way back home, but there was too much bombing outside. It hadn't stopped since I'd arrived. Another problem was that I had no idea where I was. I also did not know what was out there. I could leave and end up in a worse place than this. I knew that the south was littered with mines, left over from when the Israelis occupied the area. I had seen dozens or even hundreds of pictures of little kids whose faces had been disfigured, whose legs or arms had been torn off, simply because they had stepped on or picked up objects that looked like dolls and toys. I know enough not to pick up anything from the ground, but what if I step on something? It wasn't late, but it was already dark outside.

I weighed my options. What would Jeddo have done? What would Marc do? What would my father have wanted me to do? I wanted to be brave, I really did, but at this point, I didn't even know what brave meant. Whether it meant leave or stay.

I heard footsteps outside my door. I froze. The footsteps stopped. I stared intently at the doorknob for what seemed like forever. I sat motionless, ears perked, eyes wide. I heard the footsteps receding, but I stayed staring at the doorknob, just in case. I felt my heart was about to burst out of my chest.

I clutched my bag. I heard the footsteps approaching again. They stopped again. The doorknob turned. The door inched open. I stopped thinking. I flew out the window. I didn't care about the bombing outside. I didn't care about landmines. I didn't care about foxes or hyenas or things that might go boo in the night. The only thing I cared about was not seeing who was at the other side of that door.

I ran and ran. I am a strong runner. I was concentrating so hard on running that I didn't notice that the ground shook under my feet as a blast of wind tossed me forward. I flew up high in the air, and when I landed with a thud a few yards away, my first and only thought was that I'd tripped.

And then I was there no more.

Michael

I came to with a ringing in one ear and a buzz in the other. I couldn't hear anything else. My head lolled from side to side, and I was lying on something soft. I was in a moving vehicle, a van.

There were two pretty girls in the back of the van who didn't seem much older than me. University students, I guessed. They both looked concerned when they saw me awake, and they spoke, but I couldn't hear what they were saying. I closed my eyes, and they kept tapping me on the cheeks to wake me up. One of them put a cloth to my forehead, and the other cleaned my face. It hurt. I just wanted them to let me sleep.

I realized I was lying on one girl's lap. I looked up at her, and she was speaking to me. She was beautiful. Her eyes seemed to occupy most of her face and she had a tiny nose with tan freckles on it. Her light brown hair was tied in a ponytail, but wisps of hair flew around her face. The back of the van was open, so it was windy. She tucked her hair behind her ear, and I could see that she was saying something to me. She looked frightened. I couldn't hear her, and I put my arm weakly up to my ear to try and explain that I couldn't hear her. Her lips moved more slowly then, and I could make out that she was saying "*shou ismak*?" (What is your name?)

"Michael," I answered. "I need to call my mother. Please. I need to go home."

I don't know how long I was out the second time. I woke up in a room and could hear a lot of commotion outside. Young men and women moved frantically in and out of my room and between the other rooms. The ringing in my ears had subsided, and I could hear them shouting to one another.

"How many boxes do you have there?"

"Does anyone know if Samir has made it through the roadblock?"

"How many vans can we expect later?"

"They're unloading them onto the truck as we speak."

"Can the truck even make it down here?"

"I seriously doubt it. There's supposed to be a fucking safety corridor, but the fuckers keep bombing it."

My head throbbed. As I stood up, I realized that I was unsteady on my feet. A guy with a chubby, friendly face and a thick moustache saw me and called out: "Someone tell Lana her boy's awake!"

"Lana, your boy's awake!"

"Lana, your boy's awake!"

"Lana, your b—"

"She's not here."

"Where is she?"

"She went out on a food delivery round."

I looked around me in a daze as everyone scuttled around. Those who didn't know what to do seemed to just turn around in place. I just stood and stared. I guessed

Lana must have been the pretty girl in the ambulance. They had obviously brought me here, to this house. A sudden feeling of loss overwhelmed me. I didn't know where I was. I didn't know what happened. Five days ago, I was trying to sneak into an 18+ party with a fake ID, three days ago, I was drinking beer with my friends, acting all grown up and trying to pick up some older girls. Yesterday, I was kidnapped, taken to the house of a warlord who knew my grandfather, escaped from the warlord's house, and now I was in this strange place. I had no idea where I was and no idea what was going on. I had no idea what was going to happen to me, and all I wanted to do was to go home, back to my world and life as I knew it. I wanted to go back home to my mother, to Jeddo, and to Marc.

Just then someone ran into the house. He had a look of absolute horror on his face.

"We have an ambulance hit!" he screamed. "Quick, two people with me, we have an ambulance hit!"

I stood there waiting for I don't know how long, not totally sure what to do with myself. I was still in a daze, I wasn't sure what had happened to me, and everyone seemed too busy to explain. There was a lull in the bombing, and it was relatively quiet. I remember my mother telling me that when she lived in Lebanon during the war, people were more scared when there was no shelling than when there was. I could see what she meant now. There is more uncertainty in the quiet. I didn't know where I was to start with, and I had no idea what was going on. No one bothered to talk to me. I guess the moment they realized I could walk and talk, they set their attention on more important things. I stayed where I was.

It wasn't too long before around eight of them ran back in. They were carrying someone on a stretcher: it was the girl who had cradled my head in her lap; Lana, they had called her before. She looked hurt.

"She needs medical attention," said the guy with the round head. "We have to take her to Beirut; we can't leave her here like this."

"But they are bombing vans and even ambulances at random!" said the other girl who had been with me in the ambulance.

"She's going to be more of a burden to us here. We can take her and this guy back to Beirut, and we'll be freer to move without having to worry about them," he pointed to me. I was going home!

At that point, a tall, lanky guy with short, curly, black hair and a three-day stubble walked in. He reminded me a lot of my chief of Scouts, and I immediately liked him. His orange jumpsuit was half unzipped, and he looked like he hadn't slept in three days. They all greeted him as Nabil.

"No one's going anywhere," he said. "They've just bombed the Saida highway, and there's a huge hole in the road. Traffic to and from Beirut has been cut off."

Everything stopped. Finally, the other girl who had picked me up—her name was Rania it seems—spoke.

"So, what do we do now? What about Lana?" she asked. She was holding her hands so tightly together I was afraid she was going to break them.

"I've sent out a request for the nearest field doctor to come and have a look at her. We have to keep her stable until then; we have no choice. C'mon, let's get a move on. Hassan, you stay with Lana." Nabil turned to go, and I felt a sudden panic at seeing them all leave

"Hey," I said. "I want to come with you. Let me come with you."

"You can't," said the guy with the round face. His name was Samir I found out. "You're not trained for anything."

"Then train me," I said. "I'm a Scout; I already know basic CPR. And I'm a fast learner."

"No, we can't, *habibi*, we don't have time to train you or anyone else, our hands are full as it is," he said.

I looked at the boxes piled in the center of the room.

"Alright," I said, "I'll just help you with these boxes. I'll help you distribute the food or anything else you need to take around. Please."

"Little man! No. You're too weak. You've just been in an explosion."

This was news to me. But I was still too dazed to grasp the concept. Nabil looked at Lana, then at me.

"Actually, you can stay with Lana, and this way Hassan can come with us. Just keep her head elevated and make sure you keep pressing hard on the wound. And whatever you do, don't move her until the doctor arrives!" With that, he pulled me by the hand and sat me down next to Lana and placed my hand on her shoulder. She seemed so fragile. I smiled at her, betraying even more fear than when I was waiting in Sir's house.

It was now my turn to cradle Lana's head in my lap.

"So," I said. "Did you hear the one about the gas canister delivery guy who was fleeing the fighting in his truck? He flicked his cigarette out the window, and it flew straight into the gas canisters!"

I kept talking to Lana for I don't know how long. I told her jokes; I told her stories of my hikes with Jeddo and movies I liked and books my mother had made me read. I told her that my grandparents in England had a huge house in the English countryside and that she should visit with me someday. I told her how my grandmother was fighting for me to go to England and stay in boarding school, and how, although I was tempted, I didn't think I could leave my mother behind. I didn't know if she could handle me leaving; I felt like I needed to stay to protect her.

I told her what it was like to grow up without a father, and she nodded feebly then. I think she understood. Maybe she had grown up without a father too, so I decided to change the subject and speak of happier things. I told her how I would definitely go to England for university. I told her funny stories about my drum teacher and my other teachers at school.

I told her how they had cancelled our end-of-year school party this year because one of the graduating classes had almost killed the physics teacher by simultaneously triggering bang snaps and party poppers in class.

"Seems they didn't know he had a heart condition," I explained. "I guess you had to be there."

I told her of how one of my friends had been expelled for three days after our French teacher told him to leave the classroom, which directly translates to "take the door," so he had unhinged it and taken it with him. That made her laugh, but when she winced in pain, I stopped.

She then became really pale, and I worried she was going to die in my arms. Luckily, the doctor came just then, and after examining her, he assured us that she was going to be alright. He picked her up and took her to another room, and I realized then that I couldn't stand up because my legs had gone to sleep.

I thought of the people who'd done this to Lana. They were killers. For some reason, it hurt me to think that Marc had been like them at some point. That he, too, was a fighter, that he had held a gun and killed people. I hated to think that a man I admired and respected so much, a man who'd been like a father to me, should have had such a violent past. But I guess we're all violent in some way.

I remember the day I found out Marc was a killer. It was that same day when I'd caught my mother screaming in the bathroom. I was ten years old, and until today, when I held Lana's head in my arms, it was the scariest moment of my life.

I would say the scariest part was waking up and not finding my mother. I woke up earlier than usual for school and wanted to go in and spend a few minutes with her before I left the house, but she wasn't there. Her bed hadn't been slept in.

I had no idea what to do. I knew I couldn't call Jeddo because he wasn't home, so I called Marc. Marc had given me his number and told me to keep it safe in case of emergency, almost as if he guessed my mother might disappear one day.

"She's not here, Marc!" I remember screaming down the phone. "She's not here!"

"What do you mean she's not here? Who's not here?"

"Mama's not here. Doesn't look like she came home last night. I have no idea where she is. I don't know what to do." I think I'd started to cry.

"I'm coming," he said. "Get ready for school."

"I don't want to go to school," I remember saying. "I want to find Mama."

"I'll make you a deal," Marc said. "You go to school, and I will bring your Mama home."

I remember being very excited at the prospect of Marc and my mother together. He had always been so nice to me. He even seemed nicer than some of the fathers I met at my friends' houses who hardly ever seemed to smile or play with their kids. Marc played with me and took me to the movies, but what I really liked about him was that he treated me like a grown-up.

"She's with you?" I asked him.

I heard him sigh, and he seemed to hesitate.

"Yes, she's with me," he finally said. "You go to school, and I will find . . . I will bring your mother home."

But when I came home that afternoon my mother was screaming in the bathroom, and Marc was in the kitchen making coffee.

"Go tell your mother I'm here," he said. No hello, no smiles, no how was your day. Just my mother in the bathroom screaming and Marc in the kitchen. Whatever happiness I'd felt that morning at the prospect of the two of them being together had certainly gone by then.

When my mother came out of the bathroom, she was dressed in a bathrobe with her hair wrapped in a towel. She looked pale and skinny. I remember the way she looked made me want to cry.

Marc handed her the coffee and told me to go to my room.

"Don't tell him what to do!" my mother had scolded him. "I'm his mother."

Marc stared really hard at her.

"Really?" he said. "You tell him to go to his room then."

"Michael, go to your room," she said, but I didn't go. I was confused because she was staring straight at Marc yet talking to me. "NOW!" she said, and it was pretty clear to me then, so I scuttled to my room.

I couldn't hear anything, just murmurings that seemed to be getting louder. And then my mother shouted.

"Oh, really? You think so? Well, at least I'm not a killer like you!" Or something like that.

And then there was silence. I didn't dare move. I remember staying in my room until my mother called me to dinner. She had made me my favorite, plain pasta with tabbouleh.

"Michael, do you think I'm a bad mother?" she asked while I was in the middle of scarfing down my pasta. I had no idea what she expected me to answer. Most of the time, she was the kindest, gentlest person I knew, but when she got angry, I got really scared. I told her so, and she wiped her eyes and held my hand.

"I promise you," she said. "For as long as we both live, you will never, ever, ever, ever again wake up and not find me."

This moment seemed a bit too serious for me, so I thought it best to engage in conversation.

"Who says you're a bad mother?" I asked.

"I think Marc thinks I'm a bad mother, and Adele maybe," she sighed.

"Are you their mother?" I asked.

"I guess not," she smiled. "But they think it anyway."

"But not Jeddo," I said.

"No, not Jeddo, he would never think that," she said.

"I know."

Jeddo

He tried to read, but the words danced on the page. He couldn't make out one sentence of what he was reading. Layla smoked on the balcony, although he wished she wouldn't. Marc was somewhere inside, probably in Michael's bedroom. And now there was a dog, too. Many of his friends had dogs, and none of them heeled as well as this dog did with Layla, as if Layla were a walking T-bone steak. The television was on. He put the book down and closed his eyes. He was so, so tired.

Next thing he knew he was being shaken awake by Layla.

"Baba! Baba! Wake up! We've found him! We've found Michael!" The dog was barking, excited by Layla's mood. Layla and Marc were both jumping up and down in the living room. It all looked so surreal, he thought he must have been dreaming.

"He's somewhere near Aaitit. He's with the Red Cross. We have him, Baba! We have him! He's alright. He's alright." Layla jumped up and down excitedly.

It was Marc who spoke next. His face was pointed at the television.

"Where did you say he was?"

They all looked towards the television. Cars were stranded in front of a huge hole in the road. Women screamed, men raged, children cried. An old man stared blankly ahead of him.

"I don't think we're going to be able to go anywhere," Marc said.

"Nonsense," Layla said. "We'll find a road that's open."

"They're hitting anything moving that looks suspicious. Who knows what their definition of *suspicious* is?"

"Are you telling me now that we've found Michael, we can't go get him?" Layla asked.

"I'm telling you that we can't reach him by car," Marc said.

"Fine," Layla said. "I'll walk then."

All she needed to do now, Jeddo mused, was flick her hair back and walk out the door, just like she had done when she was six years old. Back then, her hair hadn't curled yet, and she held it up with a pink barrette that matched the color of the feather boa she had wrapped around her neck. She stood, all three feet, ten inches of her, in her black corduroy skirt, her pink boa, and a pearl necklace she must have taken from her mother's closet. She had blue eyeshadow and pink lipstick on, and she was wearing her mother's black patent-leather pumps. She was ready to go.

He had tried to explain to her that she couldn't go visit her mother in hospital looking like the progeny of Minnie Mouse and Olive Oyl, but she wasn't having any of it. These were her mother's favorite things, and she was taking them to her. Was he taking her to visit her mother or not?

He tried to reason with her. Maybe if she changed her clothes he would take her. He was just buying time. He couldn't take her to visit her mother; those were her mother's strict orders. But he was powerless, and he knew it. As if his wife were not headstrong enough, she seemed to have spawned a tiny version of herself. But Layla was adamant; he could take her, as is, or she would just walk.

He had had to stand stock still because if he had moved, he might have burst into tears.

"Fine," she said finally. "I'll just walk." She flicked her hair back and walked out the front door of their apartment.

He followed her a few minutes later when he had collected himself to find her still at the open gate of their building, peering left and right onto the street. She looked lost and scared. He knelt beside her and promised her that no matter what, he would make sure she would see her mother the next day. He would make it happen; he would figure out a way. Then he hugged her tight and wouldn't let go, lest she see the tears streaming down his face again.

She was two feet taller now, and something in him was happy to see the defiant, stubborn six-year-old still in her. Maybe, just maybe, she was not as broken as he had feared these last fifteen years. Maybe, just maybe, there was a chance his Layla could be strong and happy again.

Layla

Layla and Marc drove in silence. Every few minutes Layla picked up her camera and snapped pictures.

When she had first moved back all those years ago, the war had just ended, and Layla was shocked to find she had landed in a party town. The bulldozers, front loaders, and heavy trucks were on the streets, burying the war under new highways and concrete pavements, while the people were sweating it out on the dance floor. This was how it has been all throughout the war, Zeina had explained to her. War is good that way, Zeina had told her; it brings people closer together. As soon as there was a lull in the fighting, people would crawl out of the shelter and onto the dance floor. It was the only way to cope.

"You should come out with me some time," Zeina had told her once, a few months after Layla had moved back. "We'll find you someone to warm up your bed in no time."

It would be the last time they spoke.

Layla had felt as if she had landed in the midst of a starved population. There were no social mores. The laws of the social contract had broken down during the war, and it seemed there was no way they could be repaired. People who had been killing each other only a few years prior were now clinking their glasses, drinking to a better future. They were the frogs that had been dropped into the boiling water, and they had jumped out, intact. What they didn't know was that they had jumped into a pot of cold water that had just been put on the stove.

And they danced.

She had spent the first few months trying to get settled. She opened a bank account for herself, but when she tried to open one in her baby's name so that she could receive the transfers, she was told the baby's father had to sign to open the account. "My husband is dead," she had told the bank officer, but the bank officer just shrugged. "What do you expect me to do?" she had asked her, but the bank officer just shrugged.

And the bank officer danced.

At the airport she was told that her son could not stay longer than a month on his British passport. She would need to get residency papers for him. So she went to get residency papers for him, and she was told that his father had to sign. "My husband is dead," she had explained, but the officer at the General Security offices just shrugged. "What do you expect me to do?" she had asked him, but the officer just shrugged. "I am his mother," she said, "does that not count for anything?" And the officer just shrugged.

And he danced.

She looked for an apartment to rent; her father's apartment was too small for the three of them. And when she found the one she liked, she was told the boy's father had to sign. "My husband is dead," she told the estate agent, but the estate agent just shrugged. "What do you expect me to do?" she asked, but the estate agent just shrugged again. "But I am the one paying for the apartment," she said, and the estate agent told her that maybe her father could sign.

She looked for a job. After all, she had been a management consultant at a top London firm. But as soon as people found out she had a young baby to look after, they would shrug and tell her the position had already been filled.

So she danced. She had gone to Cleo's, the *club du jour*. "My husband is dead," she had said to no one in particular. My husband is dead. She swayed to the left. My husband is dead. She swayed to the right. A bald, short man with a cigar in his left hand and a drink in his right had approached her and had started moving to her rhythm. He pulled himself close to her, feather-dusting her leg with his crotch. He had stared at her intently as she initially avoided his gaze and then introduced himself as Cleo. She admired his courage, but this was his territory. Here, on this dance floor, he was king. And if she was being propositioned by a king, then she had better act as a queen. She took a sip of his drink and a puff of his cigar. "My husband is dead," she had told him. He smiled and led her to a small room above the club room.

The room screamed burlesque gone wrong. The remnants of cigar ash that hung in the dusty crystals of the chandelier made Layla's eyes sting, and the acrid smell that emanated from the red streaked curtains almost made her retch.

As the man approached her and slowly untucked her shirt, she felt both repulsion and intrigue. His breath stank of stale cigar and years of whiskey. Yet, she was drawn by his animalistic charm. He was shorter than she was, and yet his self-confidence soared way higher than hers. He was everything Sebastian wasn't. He was ugly, repulsive even. In her previous life, she would not have given him a second of her time, she wouldn't have lasted more than a second in this room. But in her previous life, she wouldn't have had to. In her previous life, she wouldn't be here. In her previous life, she would be living with Sebastian in London, and they would be raising their child, together. In her previous life, she had a life. But her previous life was over; she was now living a new existence, and the quicker she shed her old skin the easier it would be to adapt to this new reality she had found herself in. She had traveled back in space and time to this godforsaken country, and she would now claim it as her own. In this new, dystopian dimension she would rule. She would exert control. She would kill or be killed.

She removed Cleo's hand from her breast. As she knelt, face to the wall, on the purple, tattered velvet couch and spread her legs open, she turned back to him and asked him to take her from behind.

Marc

They drove as far as they could, then parked the car in front of a police station and continued on foot. Marc hoped that the police station, while deserted, would deter anyone from vandalizing the car and stealing parts, which was common practice, especially with German-made cars.

A few miles later they were standing outside the St. George Orthodox Church in the middle of the town square of Miyeh Miyeh. Only the pigeons were there.

"Do you want to pray?" Marc asked her.

"Please," Layla said. "I gave up on that years ago." She looked around. It was nearing lunchtime, and the sun beat hard on the square. The old stone buildings seemed to blend with the ground and the sky in the glaring light.

"You know, I really must find a reference that explains the names of our towns. Can you believe we are in a town called '100 percent'? I mean, whoever thought of that? Do you want to pray?"

"Do I look like someone who prays?" Marc said.

"You must pray for something," Layla said.

"You just said you've given up on it yourself," Marc said.

"I have. But everyone else prays for something."

"You're very good at generalizing," Marc said.

"I'm very good at reading people. That's different."

"Right now, I just want us to find Michael; after that, we'll see. Maybe then I'll pray."

"What about your brother?" Layla asked.

"What about him?"

"Do you want to pray for your brother?"

"No, I don't."

"I heard you talking to my father about him the other night," Layla said.

"I don't want to talk about him," Marc said.

"Do you feel guilty?" Layla asked.

"Guilty? About what?"

"I don't know. Do you ever think that maybe you could've saved him?"

"Maybe I could've saved him?" Marc asked. "Is that something you think about?"

"No," Layla said. "Come. Let's go see who sells cigarettes here. I brought money this time."

Marc let Layla walk ahead of him. He would rather she had her back to him. If she had held his stare, he might have broken down. He might have admitted, for the first time ever, that there wasn't one day that passed that he didn't think of his brother. Not one day when he didn't feel the guilt of not having been able to save him, or afterwards, to find him. Marc remembered every word of his last conversation with his brother. He had begged his younger sibling not to go see his girlfriend. She had lived on the other side of Beirut, in Hamra. Since the fighting had broken out a couple of years earlier in 1975, Beirut had been split into East Beirut and West Beirut by what was known as The

Green Line, so called because of the wild foliage that grew in the abandoned buildings along the demarcation line. Crossing from one side of the city, the Christian, to the other, the Muslim, was a laborious and sometimes dangerous process because of the checkpoints that had been set up and the snipers who waited patiently on the rooftops of the buildings behind each side of the line. The locals called it "the confrontation line." And with good reason, because scuffles often broke out there between the various militias that ruled their respective areas on either side of the line.

Kidnappings affected the whole country but were especially prominent along the line. Beirut was split into Christian and Muslim areas only technically. Locals made this distinction because that was easier to explain to the outside world, but the reality was much more mixed. Young men and women would cross between the two areas daily, mostly to see family or friends or just to get to work. But people of all ages would wake up in the morning, shave, dress, and then disappear.

"I promise you," his brother has said. "I promise you I won't go by car. They won't stop me. I'll walk, I'll go alone, I'll behave. I won't make trouble. I'll give fake papers if they ask for them. I won't answer back."

"Alright," Marc had finally conceded. He knew better than to keep a nineteen-year-old from seeing his girlfriend. "But I go with you."

They had arranged to meet under their building and cross together as soon as Marc returned from training camp a few days later. Marc had even lied to his mother on his brother's behalf, telling her that her little boy had to go to training with him. His mother would have never let him cross. He attracted too much attention. He was too temperamental, too good-looking. There was no telling how he would react if one of the Syrian or Palestinian soldiers insulted or slapped him or even flirted with him, as was often the case.

When Marc returned from camp three days later, there was no sign of his brother. Marc had gone around the neighborhood asking about him, but no one had seen him. Finally, his friend broke under Marc's powerful grip and confessed that his brother had gone two days earlier to see his girlfriend on the other side. And that he hadn't come back.

Michael

I was starting to smell. I hadn't changed my clothes or showered since I was at Sir's house. *Allah yerhamo,* as we say. May his soul rest in peace. Jad, one of the guys here at the Red Cross, explained to me that the Israelis were bombing any building they considered was in some way related to Hezbollah. They had even bombed a dairy factory because they said the owner was a Hezbollah sympathizer who was stashing guns for them underground.

"Are we safe?" I asked, though I doubted I would get bombed twice.

"Hopefully," he said. "We have a huge Red Cross sign on our roof and around the building. That being said, that didn't stop them from hitting one of our ambulances."

I wanted nothing more than to go home. I wanted to shower in hot water and wear clean clothes and sleep in my crisp, white sheets. I wanted to lie on the couch and watch movies. I wanted to eat proper, home-cooked food. I wanted to stop running away from threatening men and exploding houses and drones. But part of me felt that I was safer here than anywhere else in the whole world. Besides, I didn't want to leave Lana.

I sat down on the floor with the others to eat. There was canned tuna and pita bread and some instant coffee and tea. The guys had stubble that was turning into full-fledged beards, and the girls' hair was getting oily. We all stank. In the second room I could see one of the girls, Rania, trying to give Lana some water. The doctor had removed a piece of shrapnel from her shoulder and said she would be out of commission for the next six months. But at least she was alive. Nabil was trying to figure out a way to get her, and me, back to Beirut.

"Next time they allow us to take supplies we'll send you and Lana back in the truck to Beirut," he said.

Nabil was a second-year medical student on a scholarship at the American University of Beirut or the AUB as it was known locally. He had been a member of the Red Cross since starting university six years earlier.

I asked him what he would be doing if he hadn't received the scholarship.

"Probably being a butcher, like my dad," he said. "I think helping him out at his shop got me interested in medicine in the first place. I'm studying to be a surgeon. What about you?"

"What about me?" I asked. I didn't want to talk about me.

"What does your father do?" Nabil asked. I was ashamed to tell him that my father was an aristocrat. That I would never have to worry about not getting an education.

"My father's dead," I said, and I stood up to remove my plate and wash it.

"I'm sorry, man," he said. "I didn't mean to upset you."

"I don't want to go to Beirut," I said. "I want to stay here and help you guys."

"No, man, listen, we've already been over this."

"Look, with Lana out you're going to need an extra set of hands anyway. Please, let me stay with you. Let me help out. This is as much my war as anybody else's."

"I think you're still shell-shocked," he said. "But you're probably right," he extended his hand up to me. "You can start by helping me stand up." I hoisted him up, and he handed me his phone.

"Here," he said, "you'd better call your mother and tell her you're not coming home. And if she's anything like mine, I don't envy you."

"No," I said. "It's okay. She knows I'm alright, doesn't she?"

And this is what I didn't say: that if I talked to her I might lose all my resolve and ask her to come get me, and that's a risk I couldn't take for her sake or mine.

———

When in a fit of impulsiveness, I had asked Nabil to let me stay with the Red Cross and help them out, I was expecting to be useful. I wasn't expecting my heart to break. I'd understood from him that only one part of Beirut was being shelled: the southern suburbs. The rest of the city was intact, except for the leaflets that were being dropped by air, warning the citizens to run away or face the imminent wrath of the Israeli air force. Meanwhile, the people who had run up to the mountains were having the time of their lives. Restaurants in the mountain resorts were full, people were singing, dancing, partying. But here, where I was, it was a different kind of fireworks.

We had gone out to scout the area and deliver much-needed food and water. I was with Rania, Jad, and Boulos. Someone else had stayed with Lana at the house. The bombing had just stopped, and we took the opportunity of the silence to move. At first, we saw no one; the streets were deserted, the houses were half brought down to the ground. Nearer the village center, I saw him. He was a fat kid, a bit younger than me, maybe twelve years old. He had a crew cut and was wearing a red and white t-shirt and blue shorts. I only remember that because I thought he looked like the French flag, a standing, walking French flag. Or maybe I remember that because he looked both horrified and horrific. His arms, legs, and face were bloodied, making it hard to discern where his t-shirt sleeve gave way to his arms. He was lying next to a woman on the ground. She had her eyes open and was staring into nothing. The boy was holding her hand to his face and weeping.

I turned away. I couldn't look.

"Help me! Help me!" the boy screamed when he saw us, his voice gurgling as it mixed with his tears. Jad and Boulos jumped out. I stayed in the van looking out the small window in the back, and Rania was in the driver's seat. I was paralyzed. Boulos checked the woman's pulse and scanned her injuries as the boy continued to beg his mother not to leave him. That's when I saw the other little boy, on the other side of the street. He had the same haircut and clothes as the first one, the same bloodied face, but he was smaller, younger. He surveyed the scene in silence. Something about the way he stood, with a finger to his mouth, woke me out of my paralysis. I walked over to him. He couldn't have been older than seven.

"Is that your brother over there?" I asked him, and he just nodded.

"Is that your mother?" I continued. He didn't answer.

"Where's the rest of your family?"

He shrugged.

"Is your father around?" I tried one more time.

"My father is fighting. He is defending the Lebanese people and liberating them from the oppressive forces of Israel and America," he recited.

I wondered how many kids would repeat the exact same phrase if I'd asked them. Meanwhile, Jad and Boulos were moving the mother onto a stretcher. And then we heard it, the low hum of the planes, and we knew that it would turn deafening in just about four seconds.

"Come on, come on! Everyone in the van! Everyone in the van!" shouted Jad. I grabbed the boy and pushed him into the van. We all huddled as the van sped away as fast as it could go. All around us, we could see nothing but dust, and I didn't know whether it was from our tracks or from the havoc that was now being wreaked onto our surroundings by the planes. I sat next to Boulos on one bench, and the two boys sat facing us. Their mother lay on the floor. Boulos took out a white sheet and covered her and I could see the little boy cry silently as he did so.

Never in my life had I missed my mother as much as I did in that moment.

That night I lay on my cot and stared at the ceiling for a long time. The boys were sleeping in another room. Their mother had been taken to a makeshift morgue in a nearby town. I wondered what would happen to them now. Probably they would go live with some family member somewhere eventually. I found myself praying that they had family in another country, a place where they could grow up feeling safe and secure. A place where they wouldn't have to face a horror like holding your mother's hand while she dies. A place where you did not have to be subjected to other people's greed and lust for war.

And for the first time ever, I wondered if my mother had made the right choice moving back here from England and if I should seriously consider moving back.

Layla

I need to pee," Layla said. That her language had already regressed and taken on primitive undertones after only a day out in the wilderness was not lost on her. Or maybe she had been out in the wilderness a lot longer.

"You can go there behind those trees," Marc said. They were out of the village now and were crossing through a nature preserve as a shortcut to the next village.

"We'll need to find a place to sleep," Layla said.

"I reckon we have two hours before we reach the next village. We'll find a place there."

"Okay, don't look," Layla said. She gave him a peck on the cheek and spent her squatting time wondering what the hell she had just done.

In the village, an old lady had converted her home into a guesthouse. Her face was full of wrinkles, and some of her teeth were missing. She looked like she had been born in the age of the turtles but still had a glint in her eye when she spoke. She apologized to them for having only two twin beds in her guestroom and not one big one. Layla realized that to outsiders she and Marc must have looked like a couple. Layla was thankful that the woman, Marianna, didn't speak much but murmured to herself quite a lot.

It was already evening, and the cicadas were singing. Layla and Marc sat on the concrete front stairs of the house. The old lady sat on a rocking chair in the front garden under a loquat tree. She had fallen asleep under her crochet cover, hugging a picture of a young couple in their wedding attire. The young girl in the picture looked like a much younger version of the old woman. The evening was hot and humid, and Layla didn't want to eat.

"You need to eat," Marc said. "Or you won't have strength to walk in the morning." He took a bite of his omelette cooked with fatty lamb meat.

"I'm not hungry," Layla said.

"It's not about hunger, Layla. It's about energy."

"I can't," Layla said. "I can't eat knowing Michael might be hungry. I can't eat knowing he's in danger or worse—"

"Don't say it," Marc said.

"Do you think there's a chance your brother is alive?" Layla asked.

"Why do you keep bringing him up?"

"How come you don't look for him?"

"You think I didn't look for him? I looked for him everywhere. He didn't show up to his girlfriend's house. None of his friends knew anything about him. No one saw anything. No one heard anything. No one in our neighborhood had seen or heard what had happened to him." Marc snorted. "You really think I just left it like that?"

"No, I didn't mean that," Layla defended herself. "I meant why don't you officially look for him? Like why don't you go to the government or some association or something like that?"

Marc smiled.

"For someone so smart, you can be terribly naïve. There's no government taking care of this. There's nothing! This government can't even take care of its living, and you want it to take care of the missing?"

"Do you think I'm a bad mother? Do you think that's why Michael left?" Layla asked.

"No. Of course I don't think you're a bad mother."

"Why would he leave then?"

"Is there something specific you want to hear?" Marc asked.

"What do you mean?"

"You know what I think. Do you really want my honest opinion?" Marc asked again.

"No," she said. "Come to think of it, maybe not."

"For what it's worth, I think you are one of the most loving people I know. But I think—"

"What?"

"Come on," he said. He slapped her on the thigh and stood up. "Let's go to sleep. These mosquitoes are eating me alive. You have to promise me to eat in the morning, Layla. Promise me."

"Tell me what you wanted to say."

"Tomorrow," Marc said. "If you eat, I'll tell you."

In their bedroom, Layla pondered the idea of taking off her jeans and bra to sleep in her t-shirt and underwear. Normally, she had no issues taking her clothes off. She looked sideways at Marc to see if he was undressing, but he just plopped on the bed fully clothed so she did the same. Just a few minutes had passed when she could hear the gentle purr of his snoring. Despite her fatigue, she tossed around. She was bothered by the heat, she told herself, not by the nagging desire to jump into the bed next to hers and wrap herself in Marc's arms. She undid her bra, gently, silently, slipping it from under her t-shirt and placing it on the wicker chair next to her bed. She didn't dare take off her jeans. She thought of Sebastian; maybe she would dream of him. She distracted herself by remembering the first time she and Sebastian had made love, how quiet it had felt, how gentle he had been, how he had held her back so firmly with his large hands. She didn't realize that she was drifting off to sleep, just like she didn't realize that Marc was looking at her from the bed across from hers.

———

When Layla woke up, Marc's bed was empty and had already been made. She found him in the kitchen deeply engrossed in conversation with Marianna, a cup of tea in one hand and a labneh sandwich in the other. As Marianna told him about her own special technique for making clarified butter and how she cooked only with it and nothing else, as had her mother and her mother before her, Marc listened and looked with such intent as if at that moment only clarified butter mattered. Layla felt a pang of jealousy that she quickly tamed.

"But what?" Layla asked him.

"But what, what?" Marc asked.

"I'm a good mother, but what?" Layla asked.

"You're still thinking about that?" He offered her his sandwich. "Eat first."

"I'm not hungry," she said.

"Maybe your mind isn't, but your body is. Here, take a bite of my sandwich."

"Tell me what, and I'll have a bite," Layla said. The old lady handed her a cup of hot sweet tea, and she thanked her.

"How did this situation turn around like that?" Marc asked.

"Maybe I'm too clever for you," Layla said.

"Maybe you're too clever for you even," Marc answered. "Come, let's go outside." He offered her his sandwich again but she waved it away.

"But what?" she asked, once outside.

"Alright. If you insist. I think you're scared, so you're overprotective, I don't know." He took a sip of his tea, maybe to protect his face from an imminent slap.

"Listen here, Freud, after all I've been through, *scared* is not a word I would associate with me, one. Two, you can't know what it's like being the only parent to a teenager—"

"But you've always coddled him, not just now. Give him some space. Let him go. Let him find himself. And then maybe—"

"Maybe what? Say it."

"Maybe then you can also find your way back to yourself," Marc said.

"That's something you're pretty good at, huh? Finding people?" Layla walked further out into the garden, more out of shame and guilt at what she had just said than out of anger.

"I'm sorry," she said to Marc when he had followed her. "I didn't mean that."

"Layla, I know you're angry. I've been there. You're angry at your father, at me, at the world. I just wish you would trust—"

"I'm not angry at the world," she scoffed. "I think the world is angry with me. It took away my mother, it took away my home, it took away my childhood, it took away my husband, and now it is trying to take away my son. The world is taking everything from me, Marc! I'm not doing anything to the world, Marc; the world is fucking with *me*."

"But you're angry at me. Why? What have I ever done to you?"

And what Layla couldn't tell him was that, precisely, he had done nothing to her. He hadn't taken advantage of her when she had plainly asked him to, and he hadn't let her use him. He hadn't let her rule. He hadn't let her charm him, consume him, and throw him out. She couldn't repulse him. He hadn't been reviled by her. Instead, he was attracted to her. He wanted to be with her. He wanted to look through her. He wanted to help her. He wanted to see her, and by doing that he had left her raw and exposed.

"Of course I'm angry at you; I'm angry at all of you! Why shouldn't I be? My mother left me very young, my father sent me away, my husband didn't let me go with him to the concert, and my son has decided to play Magellan in the middle of a war! And you! Why couldn't you just be a bastard like all the other men in this country? Why couldn't you just leave me and my son alone? Why did you have to care so much?"

"Because I love him," Marc said. "And because I—"

Layla stiffened. "Just—just don't go there. Come on. We should go."

"Why? What is it?" Marc asked.

"Just, don't."

"What happened to you Layla? Why do you make it so hard for people to care for you?"

Layla sighed.

"Because it hurts too much," she said.

"Yes. You're right. It does. And that's what makes it so worth it," Marc said.

"You know, the night Sebastian was killed, I was supposed to be with him. But we'd had a fight. I don't even remember was it was about. It couldn't have been that important. But I was young and impulsive, and I probably started it. He was upset and asked me not to go. So, naturally, with my pride and ego in the way, I didn't. And I can't stop thinking, I can't stop wondering, if we hadn't fought, if he had let me go to the concert—"

"Don't do this to yourself," Marc said.

"I can't bear it if the same thing happens again. I can't, Marc. I'm so scared. I'm so fucking scared."

Marc hugged her tightly.

"Don't be," he said. "I'm here. Everything's going to be alright. You'll see. You'll see."

He kissed her forehead.

"Now, eat your sandwich, and let's get going. We have a long walk today and we're getting closer to the bombing. We have to be very careful. I'll go pay and say goodbye."

"Do you really love me, Marc?" Layla asked to his back.

"Technically, I didn't say it."

"Do you?"

"Shut up and eat."

Michael

The man who walked into our safe house said his name was Moussa. He was from the nearby town of Maaroub. At first, we couldn't understand what he was saying. He walked in, knelt to the floor, and started kissing Boulos's feet.

"Help me," he cried. "I beg you. Help me."

Boulos gave him some water and sat him down on a wicker chair. The man was crying so hard he couldn't speak. His face was dark, with deep lines running from his forehead all the way to his chin. He reminded me of Jeddo, but then he said he had little kids, which I thought was very strange. He seemed so old. Some of his teeth were missing. In between sobs, he explained that he had been walking a whole day to get to us, that he was the caretaker of an orphanage, that since there was a lull in the fighting, he had gone to buy bread. It was the first time bread had been available for a whole week. His family had been sheltering in the basement, he said, and then he couldn't continue. He started crying again.

"Help me!" he pleaded to Boulos. "I can still hear them; I can still hear them."

Boulos just stared at the old man, wide-eyed, shaking his head. We had just been discussing how hard it had been to get to the wounded because we had to get permission from the Israeli forces lest they bomb us. While they would not bomb cars and vans directly, they would bomb all around them to intimidate anyone moving. Boulos assured Moussa that we would get to them as soon as we could. What we didn't know at the time was that the building that Moussa had been talking about had been completely obliterated. We couldn't get to the orphanage until the next day. By the time we got there, having successfully avoided the bombs that fell on either side of the road, there were no longer any cries or screams.

Moussa stared at the rubble in front of him in disbelief. And so did I. I couldn't imagine that there were people under there, I just couldn't. Moussa ran to the heap of rubble and started removing what he could carry. Boulos and I had to pull him away together. He begged us to leave him there, leave him to die on top of his family.

"I have nothing to live for," he cried. "I have nothing to live for. Leave me here. Leave me here."

That night I lay on my cot staring at the ceiling, as I often did these days. I thought of Moussa. We had driven him to a nearby UNIFIL camp so they would keep him safe. I wondered what all these people were going to do. Where would they go? How would they live? Moussa had lost everything—his home, his wife, his children, his work. Maybe he was right. Maybe he didn't have anything to live for.

I thought of Jeddo. My Teta had died, and then he had to send my mother off to boarding school. My mother had always blamed him for sending her away. He had removed her from everything she had ever known and loved and sent her somewhere in the English countryside with nothing but horse's dung to fill her nostrils. But what about him? Did he feel like this old man did? And then I remembered what Jeddo had said about my mother crying when I was born. She was crying for herself, not for happiness and not for anyone else. It's not the cat. It's never the cat.

My mother always talked about death as a long-time companion. She told me how sad she was that I had to experience the death of my father when I was so young. But I hadn't really seen death. I'd lived with it but had never experienced it. I didn't know what death was until now. I'd never been consciously afraid for my life until now. I hadn't really been conscious of anything. Parties, porn, school, sports, hanging out with my friends, that's pretty much what my life was about. Would I ever go back to being so carefree? Would I ever be able to get the picture of Moussa out of my head?

"People forget," Jeddo had said. "They have to."

"But they shouldn't," my mother had shouted. "If people forget, then they will do the same thing all over again!"

My mother had been shocked when she moved back to Beirut because no one behaved as if the country had just gone through a devastating war.

"People danced," she said, incredulous. "People just fucking danced. Dinners, parties, people wearing the latest trends, women carrying the most expensive bags," she said. "If you didn't know there was a war going on, you certainly wouldn't have guessed it looking at people."

"In this country, we will keep doing the same thing again and again until no one is left to forget," Jeddo said.

Despite her words, my mother also forgot, and soon enough it was she who was going out to parties and dinners and coming home late and sometimes not at all. Soon enough she was dancing, too.

Marc

I never did thank you for coming with me," Layla said to him. "I really appreciate it."

They had been hiking a few hours already, and Layla had seemed calmer, despite their getting closer to the heart of the fighting. They were heading to the village of Zefta where a soldier with whom Marc had fought now lived. He thought they could stay with this friend before their final leg.

Marc smiled.

"In fact," Layla continued, "I've never thanked you for everything that you've done, that you still do, for Michael."

"He's a great boy. I love him like I love my own daughter. He has a great head on his shoulders. It's sad, if you think about it, that neither he nor Chloe had a sibling to grow up with."

"Why do you say that?" Layla snapped.

"Nothing. No reason. Just making a comment."

"What's the point? You had a brother, and now you don't. Now you're an only child. Like Michael. Like your daughter. Like me."

"Relax," Marc said. "No need to get so defensive. I'm just stating an opinion. Sorry."

Then he remembered another time he had gone to pick Layla up. The address she had given him was in a narrow street in Hamra.

"Don't come up," she had insisted, "I'll meet you in the street. And, Marc, please don't tell anyone, especially my father." When he arrived, he had found her standing at the corner of an empty street, under a rusted metal sign that read: Dr. Mohammad Hatoum, Obstetrics and Gynecology. The building looked dilapidated, and the shutters looked as though they had been either green or blue at some point but now they were just gray. Whoever that Dr. Hatoum was, he certainly didn't look like he was at the forefront of the field of obstetrics and gynecology. Layla had looked pale and tired and so sad that he hadn't dared ask her why she had been here or what she had done.

Now he realized he had probably guessed all along.

"Layla, that time I picked you up from that decrepit doctor's office—" he wasn't sure he dared to ask her now even.

"Which doctor's office?" Layla asked.

"The one in Hamra."

"I don't remember."

"Dr. Hatoum something."

"I don't know what you're talking about," Layla said.

"That place just off Souraty Street. I think it was like four or five years ago."

"Dammit, Marc, I said I don't remember, okay? Why are you insisting? What does it take to shut you up?"

"I'm sorry," he said.

But it was too late. Layla had already sped ahead of him. Why had he pushed her like that? What was he hoping to get out of this conversation? He wasn't sure.

When he could no longer see her in front of him, he quickened his step to catch up with her. He thought he could hear the sound of pine needles being stepped on.

"Layla!" He called out. "Layla, hold up!"

He ran a little faster but he still couldn't see her. He stopped. The steps he had been hearing had been his own. For a brief moment there was total silence, and then the space was filled with the whooshing of bombs overhead. The sound was so familiar, so embedded in his brain that he reacted quickly. Without thinking, he hunched and covered his head, walking like a duck to the nearest cluster of trees and sheltered between them.

"Layla!" He called out. "Layla! Laylaaaa! Laylaaaa!" He was shouting now, but his cries were masked by the low-flying fighter jets. He could feel their reverberations on his chest.

———

"Laylaaaa!"

Thirty years ago, the bombs had started raining down on their patrol while they were eating dinner. They were in one of downtown Beirut's many temples, a Capuchin church whose artworks and statues had been looted when the war first broke out. As soon as the raid had started, Marc had thrown aside his metal bowl and cup and had grabbed his brother by the arms, lifted him off the floor with the ease of a seagull scooping a fish out of water, and had run with him behind the sandbags placed under the stairs, covering his brother's head with his arms.

"See why I didn't want you to fight!" he had screamed at him over the sound of breaking windows and smashed concrete. "See why I didn't want you to fight?! Now stay! Don't move!"

Marc had run to see if anyone else needed hauling to safety. His brother hadn't stayed as instructed, of course, and when Marc had returned with another shell-shocked body, his brother wasn't there.

"Jimmy!" Marc had screamed. "Jimmy! Jimmmmyyyyyy!"

He had found him, after the raid had subsided, at the side of another soldier. He was covering the leg of the wounded soldier until help came.

That time he had found him.

Layla

She did not want to discuss her abortion; did not want to remember the huge size and coarseness of the doctor's hands, the faded paint peeling off the walls, the stench of dampness and stale cigarettes that lingered on the carpet fibers outside. Her own gynecologist had refused to perform the procedure. He belonged to a big university hospital, he explained; he had too much to risk on an illegal procedure, but he knew someone who would do it. Cash, of course.

"Don't pay any attention to the surroundings," he had told her. "He's a good doctor. You'll be in safe hands. Come back and see me when you're done, and we'll have a look-see and check that everything's in order." He was practically pushing her out the door, as if having an unwanted pregnancy in his office was tarnishing his reputation already.

She still had to pay the fee for the right to get thrown out. Still, he had been better than her first gynecologist, whom she had to pay for the right to get her breasts fondled under the guise of a breast exam.

"How old are you?" her first gynecologist had asked, while cupping both of her breasts with his stubby fingers.

"Twenty-nine," she had answered tersely.

"Your husband's a lucky man," he had said, running circles around her nipples.

"My husband is dead," she replied.

"How old would you say I am?" he asked.

If Marc wanted to hear stories about her adventures with doctors, she could tell him stories. But she wasn't up for it right now, and when he seemed to insist, she decided to walk ahead a little and give herself some space. She didn't realize that she was running, didn't notice that Marc was now far behind, didn't notice that she could no longer hear his voice. She stopped in her tracks only long enough to hear the all-too-familiar whistle of bombs falling down.

———

When she was in fourth grade, there was a boy in her class, Karim, who could distinguish different guns from the sound they made.

"This is an AK-47," he would say, as they huddled close together in the shelter. They would be waiting for their parents to arrive and pick them up, the school day having been declared over as a new bout of fighting flared up. "This is an RPG. This is an M16. This is a Slavia."

Then one day Karim did not show up to class, and they were told that he had disappeared over the weekend. At the time Layla hadn't understood what *disappeared* meant. She had missed him. He had been funny, the class clown. Where had he disappeared to? Only many years later, when she had understood that *disappeared* had been a euphemism for *died*, did she find herself wondering if he would have guessed which type of gun had killed him. She hoped her childhood friend had recognized the weapon that had obliterated him because that would have made him happy.

As she ran for cover from the bombs, Layla thought of her friend.

"This is either an F-15 or an F-16 Karim," she said to no one in particular. "See? I know a thing or two about weapons too."

It had been obvious, since the beginning of this war, that the Israeli air force was carefully choosing its targets, so far at least, so she guessed that she would most likely come to no harm. That's what her rational side figured. But the animal in her made her run for shelter, run for cover, perhaps more because of the noise than the impact of the bombs. The planes were flying very low and hitting targets that were close, and all she could think of was that she must be getting closer to Michael. She found an abandoned stone hut and rushed inside. As she sat in a corner of the empty hut alone, cradling her knees to her chest, she waited calmly to be blasted out of existence. She was ready for death, she told herself, and at that precise moment, she realized that she had never felt more alive.

When the raid subsided fifteen minutes later, Layla stepped outside to find an elderly woman baking bread on a traditional *saj*, a low, convex, heated plate of metal, heated by a gas canister on which paper-thin flat bread is baked. The woman, clad in traditional black dress and white headscarf, seemed oblivious to her presence. Layla wondered if she was dreaming. Who was this woman, and who could she have been baking bread for in the middle of a forest of pine trees? In the middle of a bombing raid, to boot.

"Come and join me for a cup of tea," the woman said, without even looking away from her bread. She was deeply concentrated on her craft.

"Who are you baking this bread for?" Layla asked her. She was incredulous at the scene unfolding in front of her and wondered whether she had passed out and was dreaming.

The elderly woman ignored her question. She told her how she was the only member left of her family. She had buried a son and a husband during the previous war, and her other son had disappeared, dragged from his home under their noses. Her daughter had married and moved to Australia a long time ago. Every few years she comes to visit, the woman said, but every time she comes, she can't wait to leave again.

"Why don't you want to send your son away?" the woman asked Layla.

"What're you talking about?" Layla asked. "How do you even know I have a son?"

"Why don't you want to let him go?" The woman asked again.

Layla shrugged her shoulders.

"He's too young," she said.

"You can be honest with me," the old woman said. She flipped the bread over for a second before she removed it and folded it in four portions and set it aside on top of a tall pile. She still hadn't looked at Layla.

"I don't know. He grew up without a father, I don't think—"

"Come on. Really."

"Maybe I don't want him to suffer like I did."

"That's not an excuse. Why'd you really not—"

"Because I don't want to live without him, okay?" Layla said. "Because I can't bear the thought of being away from him. Of missing him. I am tired of missing the people I love. Because he is all I have left."

"All you have left of what?" the woman asked.

"I don't know," Layla shuffled her feet. "He's all I have left of my dead husband. He's all I have left of love."

"Look at you," the woman said. "It is not your husband who is dead. It is you. He has moved on to another life, he is in another world. But you, you are stuck. You refuse to let him go. You have built this cocoon around yourself and your son, and you've left it there so long, you've let it harden so much that not only can no one get in anymore, you can't even get out. And you are suffocating yourself and your son. Now go, I am busy. I still have much more bread to bake."

"Who are you baking all this bread for? There's no one here."

The old woman took a batch of batter and spread it thinly on the heated dome.

"How can you bake while you have a son who's missing?" Layla pressed her.

The woman flipped the paper-thin sheet of bread from one side to the other. She looked at Layla for the first time since they met.

"How can I not bake?" the woman corrected her. "My son's fate is in the hands of Allah. Whether he is dead or alive, Allah is watching over him. But I am not Allah. And while my creator still grants me the gift of life, I will use it. And I will bake. Look at you. You are alive but dead at the same time. To die while we are living is blasphemy. There will come a time when it is your turn to die, but it is not now. It is not today. Do not die while you live, Layla. Now go. I still have much more bread to bake."

"Layla!" Marc said. "Thank God I found you!"

Layla ran to him.

"Who were you talking to?" Marc asked.

"When?"

"Now. Who were you talking to just now?"

"Now? No one. I wasn't talking to anyone, was I?"

"I heard you speaking to someone. Just now. While I was running over."

"No. I wasn't." Layla looked at the empty space around her but she couldn't see anyone. Out of the corner of her eye she thought she spotted a bird flying away.

"Did you see that?" she asked Marc.

"See what?"

"I thought I saw a crane fly away," Layla said.

"Come, let's keep going. We need to find Michael quickly, or we're going to have to check you into a mental hospital. I think you're going crazy," Marc said.

"You may be right," Layla said. "Then, again, you're not in a mental hospital. And if you managed to get away with it, then I probably don't need it."

"True. But I'm not talking out loud to imaginary cranes." Marc held her hand, and they walked on.

"Not yet," Layla said.

———

It was dusk by the time they reached the village of Zefta. Layla immediately fell in love with the area, with its red brick roofs and jasmine shrubs. The community—it was so small it couldn't be called anything else—was right above the seaside city of Saida. Layla never tired of looking out to the distant horizon to watch the sun settle for the night. Marc went asking for the house of his friend. She didn't think it would take long to figure out.

Marc and his friend Mazen hugged like two long lost brothers and immediately started sizing each other up.

"You've kept in shape," Mazen remarked, squeezing Marc's arms and slapping his flat stomach.

"It's an uphill battle, my friend. How're you doing?"

"Eh! I'm alright, I guess." Mazen looked around him, avoiding Marc's gaze.

"Are you married? Do you live alone?" Marc looked behind Mazen's shoulder as if looking to spot another person.

"Man," Mazen said. "People like us can't stay married. We carry way too much baggage. We come heavy, you know what I mean?"

Mazen looked Layla up and down. Marc introduced her as a friend and explained that they were on their way to find her son.

"How old is your son?" Mazen asked her. Marc recognized the leer in his eyes. It made him uncomfortable.

"He's sixteen. Almost. Fifteen."

Mazen whistled.

"You have a sixteen-year-old? Pretty thing like you? You've done well for yourself," he said to Marc.

Marc tried to steer the conversation away from Layla and asked Mazen what he had been up to the last fifteen years, although by his appearance he could figure that the world hadn't been kind to him. He could smell alcohol on his friend's breath and wondered for the first time if it hadn't been a mistake coming here. Mazen continued with his lewd remarks to Layla.

"Mazen, watch it," Marc said.

"What? You said you were friends. She's a free agent then," Mazen smiled. "One could lay claim to her if one wanted, no?"

Layla wanted to tell Mazen that he wasn't too bad-looking underneath his haggard appearance and that she had certainly done much worse, but she didn't get the chance before Marc had Mazen pinned on the floor in submission.

Mazen laughed.

"Angry just like your brother, eh? No wonder they took him that day."

"What're you talking about?" Marc said, releasing Mazen from his grip. "What do you know?"

"See, brother, I told you we come with heavy baggage," Mazen said. He lifted himself up and dusted his arms.

"What do you know?" Marc asked again.

"Not much. Only that he had assaulted an officer at the confrontation line. He was shoved in a car and taken away."

"Where did they take him?" Marc asked.

"I don't know. I don't know anything else. That's it. That's all I know."

"How do you know it?"

"Doesn't matter," Mazen said. "You know my daughter would've been around fifteen," he said to Layla. "Take good care of your son."

"I thought you said you weren't married," Marc said.

"No man, I said we can't stay married."

"Tell me how you know about Jimmy," Marc said again.

"There's a guy, an old man. A Syrian. Or Palestinian maybe. Not sure it makes much of a difference; they're all barbarians. Had some kind of wake-up call apparently. Found Jesus, Muhammad, whatever, who cares? He's trying to help people find out about their loved ones. The dead ones at least. Sometimes it's easier to find the dead than the living."

Layla winced.

"Sorry, darling," he winked at Layla. "Didn't mean to offend."

This time Layla shot her hand out quickly and held Marc back.

"Marc, wait, don't you want to know where this Syrian guy is?" Layla asked.

"No. I don't," he said through gritted teeth.

"He's in Beirut somewhere. Someone at the Committee for the Displaced knows him. As you can imagine, they keep him hush-hush, so you'll have to probe a bit," Mazen said.

"How do you know all this?" Layla asked.

"Doesn't matter," Mazen said. He picked up his keys and his hat. "You're welcome to my room," he said. I won't be staying here tonight. There's some whiskey in the cupboard if you want to get frisky with your woman."

It was only when he left that Layla noticed the pink baby shoe hanging from the spoiler on the back of his car. It was a common tradition in the villages of Lebanon to signal the disappearance of a child.

Jeddo

He climbed up the stairs with Miss D. He allowed himself to imagine that he would open the door and find Michael lying back on the couch, popcorn balancing precariously on his chest. Or maybe he would be in the shower, or reading on his bed, or eating a sandwich in the kitchen. Jeddo was indulging himself, and he knew it. So many times in the past, especially when Layla had been at boarding school, he had that same daydream about Layla. How many times had he climbed the stairs up to his own apartment, imagining he would find his daughter at home? How often he had prayed, walking into his empty flat, that she wasn't as lonely as he was, that she didn't miss him as much as he missed her. That there wasn't the same big gaping hole in her heart as there was in his.

He stopped at the next landing to catch his breath. He wasn't sure if it was tiredness or heartache that made him stop. Miss D barked, and he was grateful for the distraction of a door opening.

It was Mrs. Kamel.

"Hello, Mr. Kazen," she said.

"Mrs. Kamel," he doffed his hat to her.

"You know, Mr. Kazen, they don't make gentlemen like you anymore," she said.

"Call me Nadim, please."

"Very well. What brings you to our neighborhood, Nadim?"

"I'm here to get some food for Layla's dog."

"Isn't she a cutie?" Mrs. Kamel knelt down to caress the dog, and Miss D immediately turned onto her back. "I see you've spoiled her already," she winked at him.

"I've been teaching too long," Jeddo said. "I want to start having fun."

"I understand Layla's gone after Michael. I'm so relieved! I can't tell you how much I prayed for them. For you too," Mrs. Kamel said.

"Thank you, Mrs. Kamel. You're a good person."

"Nadine, please. So sorry, I forgot my manners. May I offer you a glass of water or a cup of coffee perhaps?"

"Thank you, Nadine. I'd better get a move on." He tipped his hat again. "Have a good day."

"You too."

He continued on his way up the stairs and wondered why he had said no, not to the glass of water or the coffee—those he could have at Layla's—but to the company he so craved.

Layla

She loses Michael. He is five years old, and they are holding hands as they walk in a deserted town square with a fountain in the middle. She had not felt his hand disengage from hers. She shouts his name. She shouts his name again. She looks for him in the small, winding streets leading to the square. She even looks in the fountain. Michael! Michael! Michael! This is not funny! Come out now! Michael!

Layla woke up panting, in a sweat. She patted herself down. Her t-shirt was sticking to her chest and abdomen and she was still wearing her jeans. She saw the glass that still had a few sips of whiskey sitting on the rickety wooden table by the bed. She was sweating the alcohol out. Or the nightmare. She looked around the room for Marc, but he wasn't there. He must have slept on the couch.

The night before, she and Marc had accepted Mazen's offer of the whiskey in the cupboard. Layla had spent the evening convincing Marc to leave her here and go see the Syrian man to ask about his brother, to try to find out a bit more, but Marc had insisted on staying.

"We're almost there, Layla; it's not worth it. I'm not going to leave you now," he said.

"But exactly, we're almost there, I can go from here alone, it's just a short walk away now. Go, I can manage. You should go," she replied.

But he was adamant, and she had given in, thinking that, after all, if he had waited this long, he could probably wait another few days. In two days, her life would be back in order again, and maybe, if Marc so wished, she could help him put his in order too.

She got out of bed. She was tired. Her muscles ached. She needed to get back home. She needed to get back to sleep. She would get a drink of water first. Or another sip of whiskey even. She missed her father. She thought of him going on walks with Miss D. She took off her t-shirt and fluttered it in the air to get some of the dampness out. She couldn't bear to put it back on just yet and decided that with Marc sleeping on the couch there wasn't that much risk in walking to the kitchen in her bra.

The living room was very dark. Layla crouched and felt her way in the dark to avoid hitting any low-lying tables and making a racket. She opened the refrigerator door as gently as she could, looking for water. Her hands were still quivering from her dream, and her body was shaking. Maybe whiskey was what she needed after all. Her headache told her otherwise.

"I knew about him from before," Marc said.

She instinctively slammed the fridge door and froze in place. She turned around, crossing her arms in front of her chest.

"Who?" she asked.

"The Syrian guy. Palestinian. Whatever. I knew about him from before," he said.

"Why didn't you say anything last night? You've already gone to see him?" Layla asked.

"No."

"Why not?"

Marc didn't answer, and Layla walked carefully back into the bedroom, took her t-shirt and fluttered it in the air one last time before putting it back on. She felt instantly sticky again. She flicked the light switch on in the living room, but there was no electricity. Of course, there wasn't. She felt her way to the kitchen again and rummaged around for a candle. She found one and walked back to where Marc was sitting and sat down on the couch next to him. She had left a lighter on the coffee table the night before. She felt around for it and lit the candle, walked back to the kitchen and found a small saucer. She turned the candle around to let a few drops of the wax fall onto the plate and balanced the candle into the spill. She remembered how she used to fill her hand with wax drops when she was a little girl, the short, sharp, but momentary sting of the heat on her palm, the soft feel of the wax in stark contrast to the ugliness of her hand now filled with waxy warts, and finally the pleasure and relief of removing the hardened pieces one by one.

She placed the candle on the table, and Marc passed his finger back and forth through the flame, as slowly as he could. Layla reflected on how Lebanese adolescents who grew up during the war knew how to play with candles.

"Why didn't you go see him, Marc?" she spoke gently, careful not to rattle him.

He hesitated before he answered: "I don't think I know how to grieve with dignity."

"You're talking to the wrong person," Layla replied.

"You know the problem with death?" he said. "It's the finality of it. Your inability to do anything about it. Your inability to control it, to control yourself around it. I'd rather believe that he's still missing."

"Maybe," Layla answered. "You know what I think? I think the problem with death isn't that you can't touch the person; it's that you can't feel that person's touch on you. It's not that you can't speak to them; it's that they can't hear you, they can't engage back with you. We don't miss our loved ones because we can't love them anymore. We miss our loved ones because they can't love us back. It's unrequited love. And that hurts like hell."

"So, you're saying love's a very selfish thing," Marc said. It sounded more like a question than a statement.

"Yeah, I guess that's what I'm saying," Layla said. She reached for her packet of cigarettes. She had only four left. Maybe she should save them.

"Why're you so against Michael going away?" Marc asked. "Do you really think this country is a good place for him? Do you really think he can make something of himself here? Trust me, the stories I see and hear will make you put him on the next plane out of here. Stories of drugs, abuse, neglect. We are still in survival mode all these years later. People have no moral compass. No compass generally. We can't seem to get a break. There is no stability here, Layla. Look at what's happening now. We cannot build anything lasting. Anything we build ends up destroyed."

Layla shook her head and reached again for her cigarettes.

"You know, you grow up in this place, and it frustrates you so much that you leave. And then once you leave, it somehow drags you back. And then once you're back, you can't stand it, and you want to leave again," Layla said. "I guess that's what home is."

"That's what a broken home is," Marc said. "A home is supposed to provide you with warmth and shelter and comfort and peace and love. This country is a broken home. It's better for Michael to leave now while he's still adaptable. Don't you think?"

Layla took a cigarette and put it to her lips. She lit it, drew on it, and blew the smoke above her head. "I know what you're saying is true. Every day I'm more and more convinced that he should go. It's just—"

Layla turned her head away and took another puff of her cigarette.

"Just what?" Marc asked. He put his hand on Layla's arm.

"Maybe it's the same reason you didn't go see that Syrian guy. Maybe because there are certain things you're just not ready to deal with." Layla turned to look at him. Her eyes were moist. "I just don't think I can bear the piano in the house going silent again."

"I'm here. I just want you to know that," Marc said.

She put her hand over his.

"I'm sorry, Marc. I'm sorry for everything."

Marc

The rules of war," he once read, were set to "preserve dignity in times of war and make sure that living together again was possible after the last bullet had been shot." War was not as chaotic as everyone thought. Destructive, yes. Absurd, yes. But not chaotic. First, there were the clues—often found only retrospectively—then there were the rules. Written, spoken, and unspoken rules that set basic limits on how wars should be waged.

He often thought about the last victim in a war, that person who died just minutes, seconds, before the war was declared over, just hours before the warlords sat together at a table, kissed and made up, burying their dead, dusting their sleeves, and moving on to the next conflict. He often thought of that last fallen soldier, that last bullet fired. How unlucky.

When he first met his ex-wife, they would play this game where they each tried to identify who the unluckiest person in the world might be. And the game would always end on the same note.

"I think the unluckiest person in the world is the one who hasn't met you," he would say to her. And then he would kiss her.

The rules of war, he had read, were set to "preserve dignity in times of war and make sure that living together again was possible after the last bullet had been shot." His parents had been dignified in war. His father had stopped Marc from killing himself on the roof that night and had never mentioned the incident again. In fact, he mentioned very few things again. When Marc was at home, they ate their meals quietly. His father would sit silently on the balcony smoking his pipe and listening to the radio. One night, after dinner, Marc was cleaning the dishes when he heard a thud on the balcony. His father's heart had stopped, and he had fallen off his chair. His father had lived his last years in silence and had even died in silence.

His mother had died in her sleep with rosary beads clutched tightly to her heart.

The rules of war were set to "preserve dignity in times of war and make sure that living together again was possible after the last bullet had been shot." But laws governing warfare, like all laws, were made to be broken.

He had read many books, from Sun Tzu to Vonnegut, trying to understand, or perhaps justify, his own actions. What he hadn't said to Layla last night was that he hadn't gone to see the Syrian, not because he didn't want to face the brutality that his brother may have been subjected to, but because he didn't want to face his own.

He had seen a different side of Layla last night. For the first time he could remember, she seemed calmer.

The vibrato in her voice had ebbed slightly. For the first time, she spoke openly, willingly revealing her vulnerability. She even apologized, for what he wasn't sure. She probably didn't know either. He was about to kiss her. But then she stood up abruptly and joked that there was no way she could go see Michael stinking of dirt and sweat. She apologized for leaving him in the dark and took the candle with her to the bathroom where she wanted to wash her t-shirt and underwear she said.

"It's the middle of the night," he told her. To which she replied that there was no better time, since her clothes would probably dry by morning.

"Maybe you should do the same," she said with a big smile after she pretended to sniff him.

"Do you always hide your vulnerability with a joke?" he asked her.

"Vulnerability is for wussies," she said. "I'm just happy to be reunited with my baby tomorrow. Don't read too much into it." She gave him another big smile and disappeared into the bathroom.

He gazed at the bathroom door as if he could see through it. He could hear the sound of the water as she plunged her clothes in and out of it and the sound of the soap rubbing cloth. He imagined her standing there naked in the bathroom, and for a second, he let his mind drift. He imagined walking in and holding her from behind. He imagined the warmth of her skin on his arms, the softness of her breasts. He would hold her tight and promise to keep her safe forever. He had finally found the Layla he had so desperately been searching for. He imagined her turning around to face him and encircling his neck with her arms. He felt himself harden at that point and turned his thoughts to Mazen and their fight earlier. After a few minutes the door opened slowly, and

Layla walked out wrapped in a towel. He pretended to be asleep. She blew out the candle and walked noiselessly to the room. When he woke up the next morning, she was rummaging through the fridge looking for something to eat, humming. She was fully dressed in what he assumed were cleaner clothes.

Michael

Qana. In the Gospel of John, Jeddo told me once, it is said that Jesus performed his first miracle, that of turning water into wine, in Qana, a village just a bit south of where we were now, closer to the border with modern-day Israel. I remember this story because I remember my mother suggesting we move there if it was indeed so easy to turn water into wine. She liked the idea. The Israelis, however, believe that the Qana in Galilee referred to in the Bible is actually modern-day Kafr Kanna, a village north of Nazareth in Israel. Like the origins of hummus and falafel, the whereabouts of the biblical village of Qana has been a subject of dispute for quite some time now. That's probably why the Israelis bomb the village any chance they get. And, sadly, always with the maximum number of deaths possible. Back in 1996, shortly after my mother had moved back, the Israeli Defense Forces bombed a UNIFIL compound in the village, killing over 100 civilians and injuring over

100 others who had taken refuge there to escape the fighting during Operation Grapes of Wrath.

And now they've bombed it again. Seemingly for no reason other than the sheer pleasure of it. Just like that. Because they could. Yesterday they bombed a three-story residential building, killing twenty-eight people, half of whom were children. They'd been so shocked themselves by what they'd done, I think, that they called for a two-day ceasefire as a result, and we took advantage to go down there and help. When we arrived, some villagers were already there. Some had tools for digging; others were digging with their hands. I had never in my life seen anything like it. I had seen stuff on TV, like when the buildings of the World Trade Center fell or the tsunami in the Indian Ocean. But that had been different. I had the protection of a television screen then; there was the protection of being in the safety of my own home, of being half a world away, basking in the attention of Jeddo and my mother and Marc. I was safe then. The people on TV weren't safe, but I was, and, at the time, that was all that mattered. But this was different. Seeing these people digging with anything they had, some screaming, some digging quietly, some shouting orders, and others just standing, looking, hoping, praying, being in the middle of that stirred a part of me that I had never felt before, evoked feelings in me that I never knew I had before, feelings that I cannot describe. For the first time in my life, I felt deep, deep pain, but not for myself. I wanted to cry, not out of fear but out of frustration. Frustration at this unfairness, this lack of justice, this situation that seemed out of everybody's control, this overpowering of guns and planes and metal and the frailty of human life and the lack of respect for it. For the first time ever, I was angry at my father's killer, the guy who thought he had the right to rob someone of a life, to rob a boy of his father.

I found myself wishing I wasn't witnessing this scene of utter destruction. I wished I had never asked to stay down here in the south. Yet part of me felt that this is exactly why I had stayed. I was feeling things that were so uncomfortable, so painful, and yet I couldn't believe that I had not felt like this before. For the first time in my life, I did not care who I was, I did not care where I was or where I was going. For the first time in my life, I was not Michael, I was the little boy on the street whose mother had just died; I was Moussa, the man who came to the camp crying the other day; I was the woman digging in front of me now. I was my mother; I was Jeddo; I was Adele. For the first time in my life, I was the boy who was now trapped under the rubble, the one with sand and earth in his mouth and eyes and ears. I felt like I was choking, like I couldn't breathe. And I ran. I ran with my arms and my legs flailing towards the pile of rubble, and I started throwing stones away from the pile with all the power I could muster. I wanted to free those children under the rubble if it was the last thing I ever did.

That evening Jad came to tell me that Nabil thought it may be better if I didn't go out with them on rounds anymore. That it would be better if I stayed at the camp they'd set up with the UNIFIL not far from where we were, the camp where they took the old man and the two boys. I asked him why, and he said that Nabil was worried about me. That he was worried that Qana had really disturbed me. No shit.

"I'm okay." I said. "I'm fine."

"You didn't see yourself out there, man," Jad said. "We didn't know if you were screaming or wailing. Let me see your nails. Did you hurt yourself?"

I showed him my bandaged fingers. Two of my nails had come off but the pain felt good somehow.

"I was really worried about you out there. It looked like you were having a nervous breakdown. I can't take that responsibility, you know what I mean? I can't risk you hurting yourself. It's rough out there."

I tried to smile, but my tears started falling down again. "Rough is an understatement," I said.

"Yeah, it is." He was kind enough not to look me in the eyes.

"What am I supposed to do at the camp?" I asked.

"You don't have to do anything specific at the camp. Just help out, I guess. Help out with serving meals maybe, hang around with the other people, teach the kids some English, tell them stories, things like that. Simple stuff. Listen, you've already done more than enough. Really."

"Can I think about it, or do I have to go?"

"You can think about it, but I think it's for the best. He's sending Lana to the camp also," Jad said. "There's no way she can get back to Beirut. Not now. Those guys out there are mad; I'm not sure which side is madder."

"When's Lana going to the camp?" I asked.

"This afternoon," he said.

"Okay, I'll go," I said.

Layla

Layla was sure her mind was playing tricks on her. She didn't understand. Michael was here. He was here at the safe house. That's what they'd told her over the phone. That's what the person had said.

"Your son Michael is here with us at the Red Cross safe house."

"Did I hear wrong?" Layla asked the twenty-something boy-man standing in front of her now. He had a big bush of red hair on his head and about a week's growth of beard. His name was Ziad.

"No, you didn't," he answered her. His eyes were kind and tired. So tired that they couldn't express surprise at Layla and Marc having walked all the way to get there. "We just didn't think you'd walk all the way here to find him."

"What did you think I would do? Did you think at all?"

"Layla," Marc said. "These people are trying their best."

"I understand your frustration ma'am, and I am truly sorry for the confusion," another young person with a deeper voice said. "We moved Michael to the camp after he—"

"What? After he what? What happened to him," Layla said.

"Nothing. Nothing happened to him. Nabil just felt that he was better off away from here."

"Who's Nabil? Where is he? Where can I find him?"

"Mrs. Cape, we'll take you to Michael first thing in the morning, don't worry. It's too dark now. It's too . . . dangerous." He pointed his finger to the ceiling, and Layla instinctively followed it.

"The bombing will start very soon," he said. "But I assure you Michael's safe."

"I don't think you understand," Layla said, her mind racing to find a way to explain to this boy-man that, having come this far, she wouldn't be stopped from seeing Michael now.

"Madame," he said patiently and looked at Marc as if pleading with him to drive some sense into this wild-eyed woman. "I'm the one who does understand, believe me. And when you go outside to pick up human bodies from the side of the road because people were too stubborn to listen to a curfew, you will understand too."

Layla suddenly felt every scratch she had gotten from the thorn bushes growing alongside the road. She felt every blister on her heels and between her toes opening up, every ache in her back, every muscle throbbing. She sank to the floor and hid her face in her arms. Her body heaved, and for a while she felt like she couldn't speak, couldn't breathe.

Marc knelt down in front of her and held her arms.

"I just want to see my baby," she muttered. "I just want to see my baby."

"First thing tomorrow, I promise," Marc hugged her close and whispered in her ear. "First thing tomorrow, I promise. If they won't take us, I will take you, I promise. Hush now, Layla, hush now." He rocked with her back and forth until she finally stopped shaking in his arms.

When she had calmed down, Ziad asked them to join him and the rest of the team for dinner.

"It's only canned tuna and corn," he said. "There's no bread that we can get our hands on. But we do have Arak," he said a little bit more cheerily.

After a few rounds of Arak, Layla, Marc, and the rest of the team could no longer hear the thunder of the planes flying low overhead. The bombing in the south had quieted down lately, they explained to their guests. The planes were now targeting the southern Beirut suburbs.

"People are living in the streets in Beirut apparently," said Rania, who was studying nursing at the Lebanese University. "They have nowhere to go."

"One day I will write a book about this war," Ziad said.

"More like an opera," said Rania. They all started laughing hysterically.

"I can't believe we're laughing about this," said Hisham, wiping his eyes with his thumb.

"Well, it's either laughing or crying, right? Better laugh than cry, I say. It's all stress relief one way or the other," said Ziad. He laughed and downed the remainder of his sweet anise seed drink.

"I think we better get to bed, especially if we're to take these poor parents to see their son first thing tomorrow."

Layla did not correct him.

Michael

J eddo used to tell me that you never know how important a body part is until it starts to hurt.

"Even your littlest toe is important," he said. "You just won't know how much you use it until it starts hurting."

I remembered the little boy in the mini-market under our house who only had four fingers attached to a misshapen hand—some medication his mother had been taking while she was pregnant had done this to him apparently.

"Ignorance," my mother said.

"Poverty," Jeddo corrected.

"What if it was never there," I'd asked him. "How would you know how important it is then?" To that he had no answer. But I could tell my question made him sad.

Looking at Lana trying to maneuver her way in and out of the ambulance on our way to the camp, I figured the shoulder must have been a very important part of the body because she was constantly wincing in pain. Her shoulder was held tight in a sling, but the road to the camp was full of potholes, and the van kept veering left and right to avoid them, which hurt her a lot but not as much as when the driver fell straight into them. She just screamed out in pain then.

My action was instinctive. I hopped off my bench, almost snapping my neck in two as I banged my head on the roof of the van when we hit another pothole. I sat next to Lana and moved her in such a way that her back was against my torso. I cushioned her head against my shoulder and swung my arm around to cradle her chest with both arms to hold her steady. I pinned her to me for the rest of the drive to the camp, taking in the shocks from the ride and cushioning her as much as possible. Only when we arrived did I realize that for the better part of ten minutes, I had my arm across her chest right under her breast. When, at night, I thought back on that ride and how close my hand was to her breast, I wanted to masturbate. But there in the ambulance, it had felt like the most natural thing ever. Nothing like when my friends and I tried to snoop into the lockers of the girls when we changed for gym or when we were at the pool or the beach. Or like when we eyed the girls during break time and imagined we were those studs in the porn videos. It was nothing like that.

The children at the camp made me very sad. The old people, too. But there were more children than old people. Jad explained to me that it was really hard to wrench some people from their towns and their homes, even under heavy shelling. Even when these homes were destroyed some people preferred to stay within the confines of three half-walls rather than leave their places behind. One old man said he would rather die in his home than survive in a makeshift camp. But the children came. I guess they had to. They came running at Lana and me and hugged our legs. I didn't know what to do. I didn't know these kids and didn't understand why they came running to us like that. I looked at Lana as she naturally hugged the kids back with one arm, holding her shoulder up high so as not to get hit and rubbing their heads and backs with the other. So, I did the same. But I didn't lift my shoulder because that would have looked ridiculous.

I pitched Lana's tent for her and then put up my own. I didn't have anything with me except a change of clothes I'd been given by a guy called Rami, so it was all relatively quick.

"What are you smiling at?" asked Lana.

"I'm thinking how much my mother would love to see me now, without any of my belongings," I said. "She gets upset with me when we travel because I pack half my games, my consoles, my cards, chocolates, sweets, and once I even took my skateboard."

Lana smiled.

"I didn't have that problem," she said. "I didn't really travel anywhere. We just spent our holidays up in the mountains, in my father's village."

Lana's English was not very good, but her French was impeccable, so we agreed that we would hold dual conversation classes with the children so they could take advantage of both languages. None of us had realized that what these kids needed was neither the English language or the French. They needed someone to hug them and tell them or show them that everything was going to be alright. What they needed was safety and security, preferably with as little noise as possible.

Rima had just arrived at the camp from Tyr with her younger sister. She was seven, and her sister was six years old. Her mother had disappeared with their stepfather and baby brother during the night. They had no idea where they were. During one of the conversation circles we were holding, I was sitting cross-legged on the floor when Rima walked up to me and sat in my lap. I opened my arms to allow her to snuggle in comfortably. Five minutes later she was asleep in my arms.

When I was about Rima's age, I often used to crawl out of bed to find my mother sitting alone in the dark with the TV on for company. I would walk up to her, and she would open her arms to welcome me into her lap, where I would inevitably drift back to sleep. Not once, until now, did it ever occur to me that in those moments, when my mother represented the essence of safety and security to me; not once did it occur to me that she may well have been just as scared and bewildered as I was.

Marc

He offered to sleep on the floor so she could have the cot, but she wouldn't have it.

"No way," Layla said. "An old man like you? You'll throw out your back. I'll sleep on the floor." When they couldn't agree, Layla insisted they share the mattress. But now he was eyeing the floor again as Layla tossed and turned next to him. She had fallen asleep very quickly, complaining that she was exhausted. Now she felt very warm next to him. Too warm. It wasn't that hot outside.

He could hear the quiet hum of the warplanes in the distance. It wasn't long before they got louder. They were obviously flying closer and lower. He braced himself, as he had often done in his youth, for the deafening noise of the bombing, the rumble of the earth and rock as it shook at its encounter with metal and fire.

But like a mosquito that had changed its mind, the hum abated. Maybe there would be no bombing tonight. Layla seemed to have eased off the jerking, and he felt the Arak get the better of him. When his eyelids felt too heavy, he let them close.

He wasn't sure what had woken him up: a noise, the ground shaking beneath him, or Layla suddenly jumping out of bed. Layla was pacing around the room, patting herself on the chest.

"I knew it!" she muttered. "I knew it! Bombing. Bombing. Wake up! Wake up! We have to go! Michael! We have to go! Bombing! Bombing Michael! Go. Have to go!"

"Layla, calm down! What's going on?" He could feel the walls and the ground beneath him grumble, but he couldn't hear anything. He could only hear Layla, and he had no idea what was going on.

"Bombing Michael! We have to go!" She was now screaming.

He had to get his wits together. He had to get her to calm down. But she was moving around too fast for his just awakened brain. One of the guys ran into the room.

"What's going on?" the shadow asked. "Is she okay?"

Marc finally caught hold of Layla's arms. She struggled against him.

"I don't know," he said, as he looked into her wild eyes. "She's delirious."

Layla struggled to free herself from his grip. "Let me go! Let me go!"

"Help me get her on the bed. I don't want to hurt her."

Hisham ran over to him and helped him move Layla to the bed. She was very strong, and Marc had to push hard to pin her down. He felt her forehead.

"She's burning up! We need to give her something now."

"Please," Layla whimpered. "Michael. Please. Go. Must go."

"Just calm down." He put his lips to her forehead to better gauge her temperature. "I'll go. I'll go now. Just calm down. Here, take this. We'll get you some water." He handed her the pills that Hisham had just given him and propped her up.

Finally she relented, and after several moments, she seemed to calm down. Marc sat next to her on the cot and kept holding her until she stopped shaking and fell asleep again.

"Are they really bombing?" he asked Hisham. "I can't hear anything."

Hisham shook his head slowly.

"They did a bit at the beginning of the evening, but it sounded far away. Probably Beirut again," he said. "Why don't you go sleep in my room? I'll watch over her for a while."

"It's okay," Marc said. "Thanks, you've done enough." He looked at Layla. "I don't think she'll be able to go anywhere tomorrow. She needs to rest."

Layla slept through most of the next day and the next night, Hisham again by Marc's side as he kept watch over her. Her fever was not abating, but she was refusing to take any medication, accusing him and Hisham of trying to poison her so that she couldn't get to Michael.

"Why wouldn't I want you to get to Michael?" Marc asked. "I'm trying to get to Michael just as fast as you!"

Layla simply shrugged her shoulders.

"That's why I need you to take the meds. I want you to get better so we can go."

"Nothing wrong with me," she said before she fell asleep again.

The third day was the worst. Marc and Hisham were again by Layla's bedside when Marc felt Layla's palm on his cheek.

"Seb . . . ian," she mumbled. " . . . here. You're here . . . left me . . . I knew . . . come back . . . miss you, baby." She gazed into his eyes with such recognition that Marc wondered if she hadn't been playing a trick on him.

But then she turned to Hisham and weakly reached out for his hand. "Mama."

She sniffed. " . . . both here . . . missed you so much . . . so hard, so hard." Layla turned to Hisham and said: "letter."

"She's burning up again," Hisham said. "We have to give her something stronger."

"No," Layla turned to him and said, " . . . 'm fine . . . no, Mama . . . nothing . . . don't go . . . please . . . too good . . . too good."

Marc and Hisham looked at each other, each hoping the other understood. Finally Marc said:

"We're not going anywhere, my darling. We're right here." He caressed her hand.

"How about I get us all a drink to celebrate?" Hisham asked, and he gently let go of Layla's hand. Less than a minute later he came back with three glasses of water. One had something fizzing inside.

Hisham handed out the glasses and gave the one with the medicine to Layla.

"To our reunion," Hisham said, raising his glass.

"To our reunion," Marc said, genuinely impressed with Hisham's ability to quickly assess and respond to the situation at hand.

Layla beamed at them both and accepted the drink they offered her. A few minutes later, her hands slid off theirs, and they knew she had again fallen asleep.

When Hisham had gone back to catch whatever sleep he still could before dawn, Marc stared helplessly around him. For the first time since he called Jeddo to tell him that Michael had gone missing, he couldn't remember how long ago now, he had no idea what to do.

Michael

Another day passed. I walked towards my tent. Despite the heat and dust, I was coming to terms with the camp being my home for a while. I was getting attached to these kids. I was happy to play with and comfort them when they needed it. I thought of Rima falling asleep in my lap for about an hour. I didn't dare move the whole time, and my arm started hurting. She was very small yet still managed to feel heavy. How that worked I wasn't sure. One of the nurses at the camp offered to take her from me and put her in her cot, but I didn't want to let her go. She seemed so comfortable.

"It's okay," I said, "I'm sure she'll wake up soon. She seems so comfortable. I don't have the heart."

"She seems to really like you; you're like a big brother to her," she turned and walked away.

"Nurse Adla?" I called after her. "What happens to these kids after . . . where will they go after this is over?"

She shrugged. "I wish I could tell you. We'll try to find their parents, and failing that, their closest relative."

I looked down at Rima's peaceful face. Her cheeks were flushed, and she clutched her plastic doll to her chest. I felt tears wet the face of her doll. Nurse Adla squeezed my shoulder.

"Try not to get too attached," she said.

Rima woke up. She got up without saying a word and joined the other kids in a game of tag. My eye caught Lana's, and she smiled and winked at me. I felt like the whole world had smiled at me then. After a while I got up too and joined the game.

Later that day I wanted to plan the next day's program. At least that's what I told myself. I walked towards Lana's tent in the girl's quarters. I stood outside, hesitating when I heard her grunting.

"Lana?" I asked. "Can I come in?"

I heard muffled sounds.

I felt bad for Lana; she was obviously in much more pain than she was letting on. Earlier, when we were playing with the kids, she had been putting on a brave face, I realized.

She had asked me how I was doing. How I was doing! She was the one in pain, and she was asking how I was doing.

"I'm okay, I guess," I said, packing away some of the donated toys the kids had been playing with. "It's all a bit surreal. Never thought I'd have a baby sleep in my arms since my mom pulled me out from under Jenny."

"Huh? Who's Jenny?"

So I'd told her about my friend Jennifer from play group all those years ago who would force me to play "house" whenever I went to her home for a play date.

"Her dolls were the children, and we would have to feed them and bathe them and lull them to sleep," I laughed. "I hated that game! I kept telling my mother that I didn't want to go to Jenny's house, but her only reply was that Jenny's mother was the only mother in play group that she could stomach, so I was stuck. Luckily, one day—"

Lana had started laughing.

"Man," she said. "I love your mother already."

"After we had put 'the kids' to sleep, Jenny turned to me and said: 'Now we play mommy and daddy!' and before I could ask what that was, she had me pinned in the corner of her room and was literally, I kid you not, covering my face with kisses!"

I was laughing too now and could hardly continue my story.

"Luckily," I said, "that's when our two mothers walked in on us. I don't know who was more mortified! Me, Jenny, my mother, or Jenny's mother. Later that evening after she gave me my bath—I was like six at the time—my mother finally agreed that maybe I was better off hanging out with boys."

Lana was cracking up by then, and when I saw the laughter in her eyes, I sort of wished we could reenact that scene together. It had been an awkward moment. You know, like when you catch someone's eye, and then you don't know where to look anymore?

Now, as I walked into Lana's tent, I found her stuck inside her shirt. I wasn't sure if she had seen or heard me, and I wasn't sure what to do. She was trying to pull her t-shirt above her shoulder. At the sight of her small breasts, I felt a tightness in my pants, which only immobilized me further. Lana stopped struggling. Suddenly her head popped out from under her t-shirt and she was obviously startled when she saw me. She took a step back and screamed, which made me step back and scream in turn.

"What are you doing here?" she asked. She was panting from her efforts.

"I c...c...came to help." I came to stutter was more like it!

"I don't need help! What do you want?"

I wasn't sure why she was so angry and not knowing how to react or what to do, I did the only thing I could think of: I turned and ran straight back to my tent.

I was too embarrassed to sleep that night. The image of Lana's head popping out of her t-shirt woke me up as soon as I dozed off. When morning finally came, I waited in my tent for breakfast to be over before venturing out. I just wanted the memory of last night to be over already.

When I figured it was safe to leave my tent and not have to sit facing Lana over breakfast, I got dressed, walked stealthily to the makeshift bathrooms, brushed my teeth, and slapped water on my face. The deodorant in the bathroom had run out, and I prayed they would replace it soon. I sniffed my underarms, but either they were okay or I'd gotten used to the smell of me by now.

I found Hussain waiting in front of my tent. Hussain was seven years old and missing his two front teeth. His black hair fell straight onto his dirtied face. He walked around with only one torn plastic slipper and his feet were black.

"Hey, Hussain," I rubbed the top of his head. "No one's brought you shoes yet?"

Hussain shook his head slowly.

"Hopefully, today," I said. "What's that in your hand?"

Hussain offered me the cheese sandwich and orange juice he was holding.

"Is that for me?"

Hussain nodded.

"From Lana," he said and handing over his booty he turned and ran back towards the group. One day, I thought, I'd get this boy to say more than two words to me.

I busied myself with the construction team all morning. There was still no sign of the bombing letting up. No one had any idea how long the war would continue or if it

BIRDS IN THE RAIN

might drag into the winter months. In just a few weeks the rains would start, and we had to be ready for any eventuality. So, I spent the morning mixing cement. It reminded me of that Bob the Builder program my mother let me watch when I was young. Bob the Builder, can you fix it? Bob the Builder, yes, we can!

But at lunchtime Lana came and sat right next to me. I cursed again that there was no deodorant in the bathroom this morning.

"I saved you some breakfast this morning," she said. She was in a cheerful mood.

I nodded my thanks.

"Peace offering," she said.

"Thanks," I said, still not looking Lana in the eye. I was tongue-tied, not unlike Hussain earlier.

"Listen," Lana said, leaning closer. "I'm sorry about last night. I didn't mean to snap. I was just in so much pain. It's been so painful I've had to sleep with my clothes on the last couple of nights."

"Why don't you speak to somebody? Get checked out," I asked my plate. Jeddo wouldn't have approved. You never ever speak to anyone without looking them straight in the eye, he always said, regardless of age or gender or circumstance. Looking someone in the eye when you speak to them tells them not only that you respect them but that you respect yourself.

I stood up to leave. I told her she should get one of the other girls to help her. Or Nurse Adla.

"I was wondering if I could ask you to help me change tonight," she said.

I nodded quietly, as I felt the blood rushing through my body, including all the places it shouldn't. I prayed to God above that she didn't notice anything. Lana stood up and asked me if I would be joining the group this afternoon. I poured more water into my glass and pretended to drink it.

"I'll finish the wall I'm working on and I'll join you later," I said, feeling elation, relief, excitement, embarrassment, joy, and apprehension all at the same time.

I couldn't concentrate on my job all afternoon and quite a few times slapped double the amount of grouting necessary between the bricks.

When the dinner bell finally rang, I was the first at the table, before some of the kids even. But after I had piled my plate with lentil and rice stew and salad, I realized that I wasn't that hungry. I had to bribe some of the older boys to eat my food so that I didn't waste it. I promised them that if they ate my food, I would give them my share of juice and cake for the next few days. It worked. I kept eyeing Lana, who was sitting at another table. She seemed to be eating just fine. When she finally finished and had taken her plate to the trays on the side, she smiled at me and motioned for me to follow her. I bid my little friends goodnight and promised them new games the next day.

But once in Lana's tent, I froze. I realized I had no idea what to do. All this anticipation, and now I didn't know what to do. I remembered Jeddo telling me once that the shortest distance between two points was a straight line, and I decided to apply this to my current situation by asking a direct question.

"What do you want me to do?" I asked.

Lana had finished lighting her candles, and she came and stood in front of me. Then she turned her back to me and asked me first to take off her jacket, gently. I held her jacket by the collar and slid it gently down her arms. She turned back to face me.

"Now's the tricky part," she said. "You need to take my t-shirt off without me having to move my shoulder."

I held her t-shirt from the bottom and started pulling it straight up.

"Ow, ow, ow, ow, ow," she said. "Gently, gently."

In my eagerness, I was almost yanking her t-shirt off.

"Sorry," I said, as I tried again. This time I pulled her t-shirt up halfway only. I took her uninjured arm and pushed it gently through the arm hole. The t-shirt now hung from her neck on one side and I could see the underside of her breast.

"I'm not wearing a bra," Lana said, as if to warn me. "I can't strap it on."

I tried not to look, but it was impossible.

"Have you ever undressed a woman before?" she asked me.

I didn't answer as I slowly pulled the t-shirt around the side of her head, stretching the material. When the t-shirt was hanging only from her injured shoulder, Lana tilted her head and smiled at me. Her breasts had now come into full view. They were small and firm and the most beautiful thing I had ever seen. I was ogling, and we both knew it.

"Well?" she asked again. "Have you?"

"No," I lied. I did not want to tell her of the time I had to undress and put my mother to bed. The last person I wanted between us in this tent right now was my mother.

"No, I haven't," I said. As I gently pulled the t-shirt down over her injured shoulder, something other than her breast attracted my attention, and I couldn't help staring at her wound. Beneath the gauze the scab was too obvious, and the skin around it was all red with spots of black. It was scary. I tried not to look too worried.

"Your wound's infected. Why didn't you tell anyone?"

"Ssh, don't shout. It's fine, really. It'll be okay in a few days."

I instinctively put my hand to her forehead, but she didn't have a fever. It's what they used to do to us in Scouts camp if we got hurt. But not one of us ever had a wound this huge. Of course, we had never been shot at or involved in an explosion before.

"It's not fine!" I said. "Lana! You should know better than to ignore something like this."

"Michael, there are people here missing whole body parts. There are orphaned babies. You really think I'm going to bother them with my slightly injured shoulder?"

"No, you're right," I said, pretending to agree. "Don't tell 'em. I will!" I turned round to leave. I needed to find someone to look at Lana's shoulder.

"Michael, wait!" Lana called from behind me. "Stay. I'll show it to someone tomorrow. I promise. Please stay. Stay with me."

When she saw me hesitating, she said: "Kiss me."

I knew Lana was using delaying tactics for reasons I couldn't understand. I also knew that a half-naked woman who's been driving me crazy has just asked me to kiss her and that I would be stupid to refuse. Besides, who knew what was going to happen? We might all be bombed to oblivion by tomorrow. Did I really want to die a kissing virgin? But I'd never kissed anyone before, and I wasn't sure I wanted to show Lana how inexperienced I was. But before I knew it, Lana had put her lips to mine and gently pushed her tongue into my mouth. I let my tongue play around hers as I closed my eyes to savor this moment. I was, at that moment, by far the happiest I'd ever been. I raised my hand and held it in front of her breast, but I didn't dare touch it. Lana took it and placed it on her breast. As I felt her nipple harden and the soft skin around it, I suddenly felt a bit of warm liquid in my crotch and I immediately froze again.

"I've got to go," I said.

"Michael," she called after me. "Please tell no one about this?" she begged.

"You bet!" I said. And I ran.

Michael

Back in my tent, I replayed the scene with Lana over and over again. I wanted desperately to go back to her, to hold her breasts, to kiss her all night. I wanted to be close to her, to feel her skin on mine. I was so wrapped up in my thoughts that I didn't hear the planes approaching. The bombing caught me by surprise. It was so loud! The planes sounded close to us, so close I thought they might bomb us too. My first thought was to go back to Lana's tent, to make sure she was okay, that she was covered with something in case she had to run for shelter. But as I was leaving my tent, I saw children running towards me, screaming.

"Micol! Micol!" I hugged as many of them as I could and led them into my tent.

"Shh, it's okay," I said with so much calm that I surprised myself. "It's okay," I said, as I ran my hands over their hair. "It's okay. It's gonna be okay. Hush, hush."

Two minutes later, the raid was over. I sat cross-legged in the middle of my tent surrounded by seven or eight children. Some kids were quietly whimpering. Others were shivering. They had their arms around my neck and shoulders.

I suddenly realized these kids trusted me to keep them safe. They believed that by hanging on to me they could keep danger away, that I could save them from being hurt and perhaps from dying. To these kids right now, I was the most important person in the world. I wished I was a swan and that I could open my wings wide and protect them all under my warm soft feathers. I stood up and ushered them all to my bed and instructed them to sleep sideways so they could all fit, and then I lay down on the floor next to them. I closed my eyes. I wanted to dream of making love to Lana, of being away from here, and of all these kids being grown up, living happy lives. I wanted to dream of all of us living happy lives.

When I woke up, all the kids had gone. I checked my watch. I was late, so I got dressed quickly. I decided to brush my teeth and wash my face after breakfast. When I got to the canteen, one juice and one lonely sandwich were left at one of the tables, and I sat down to eat. I usually didn't like eating alone, but I didn't mind it at all this morning. On the contrary, I was quite happy with the solitude. My thoughts drifted to Lana and the night before. I wondered if she realized why I'd left so abruptly. I decided to behave as if nothing happened. Maybe tonight I could see her again, and this time I could control myself. I wondered what Marc would say if I told him. I hadn't thought of him in several days. I hadn't thought of Jeddo either. How could I not think of them? How long had it been? I couldn't even remember. I had been busy with the kids. Every day, new kids came to the camp. They were scared and vulnerable, and they needed our attention. The ones who were already here were getting so rowdy and agitated that yesterday Lana and I had to set some rules with them. No fighting. No swearing. No interrupting and no playing harshly were the rules we started with. The kids seemed okay with it so far. I realized now that while I didn't necessarily miss my old life, I did miss my family, and I knew they deserved better than me not thinking of them. I didn't know when I was even going to see them again, and yet, somehow, right now that didn't seem to matter. I was happy. It was weird, but I was happy. Despite all the misery I saw around me, I was happy.

"Jan wants to see you. ASAP." It was Mohammad, one of the older camp volunteers. I panicked. He must know something. Someone must've seen me go into Lana's tent. Now what?

"Okay sure," I said. "Thanks." And then, "Do you know why?"

"No. What's that stupid smile on your face?"

"I don't have a stupid smile on my face."

"That's what you think," he said. He winked at me and left. I finished my juice and went to see the director. I was sure I was in trouble.

"What's that stupid smile on your face?" was the first thing the director asked me when I walked into his office in a makeshift container. Some squares had been sawed into the sides to let air and light in, and now a sun ray hit my eyes and I had to squint.

"I don't have a stupid smile on my face," I said. "I'm squinting. Because of the sun."

"Stand here," he said. "Yeah, there. See? Now there's no sun hitting your face, but you still have a stupid smile on your face. Are you in love? You should be careful. In war situations, all emotions are heightened. Misery can intertwine itself with elation so finely that one can no longer tell the difference." That's it, I thought; I was getting kicked out. I really couldn't get why he was talking to me about love when the country was at war. Only last night I thought our camp was going to get bombed; what was this guy so chirpy about? Surely we had important things to worry about.

"You're in a good mood this morning, Sir," I said, this time smiling for real. "Is the war over? Am I missing something?"

"The war isn't over yet. But it is for you. I have some good news."

"What?"

"I'll be really sad to lose you. You've been absolutely brilliant with these kids. Never thought a fifteen-year-old would have it in him to take such good care of little rowdy orphans. But you, you're a natural. We'll be sad to lose you, but I'll be happy to have one less person to worry about."

"Where're you taking me?" I asked.

"Me? Nowhere. Your parents are coming to pick you up."

I didn't know what to think. Different emotions flooded my brain. Relief that he didn't in fact know about Lana and me, confusion at the word *parents*, since I had grown up with "your mother" or "your jeddo," never "your parents." I assumed he was mistaken, and realized, much to my amazement, that I hoped he was.

"My parents?" I asked. "Are you sure? How did they even get here? I thought you said all the roads are closed."

"I dunno," he said, gesturing with his hands. "We got a message over the radio this morning that your parents were at the safe house and that they were coming to pick you up today—as soon as the situation allows, that is."

"Okay, thank you."

I didn't want to confirm that my mother was coming to pick me up. I missed her terribly, but I did not want to leave. Not now. I hoped that they had confused me with someone else. Now all I had to do was wait and see who that mysterious couple was and why they were coming here. As I stood outside the container in the morning breeze and sunshine, I found myself hoping against hope that it wasn't for me.

I walked over to where the kids were playing. I quickly surveyed the scene to make sure there was no fighting. One group were drawing a hopscotch grid on the ground; another were chasing each other in a game of cops and robbers. A group of older kids were playing football with a deflated ball. I looked around for Lana but couldn't find her.

"Where's Lana?" I asked, but no one answered. They were all absorbed in their activities. I grabbed Hussain by the shoulder as he whizzed past me. "Where's Lana?" I asked, but he shrugged his shoulders and kept going.

"She went back to her tent," said a small voice behind me. It was Maha. Maha was around ten years old and had been brought to the camp with her sister yesterday. They'd been found in a hashish field, shivering in stunned silence. When the Red Cross volunteers couldn't get a word out of them, they moved them to the camp while they searched for their families. As far as I knew, these were the first words that any one of the girls had uttered.

"Why did she go back to her tent?" I asked her, but when she simply stared at me, I realized that was the end of our conversation. I decided to just wait and see. Maybe she had forgotten something in her tent.

"Alright, everyone," I clapped my hands. "Circle time!" I gestured for Maha and her sister to join us.

"Why don't you come and sit next to me?" I said. "And you can tell me about you." Although I wondered if I could hear another horror story of girls and boys being raped, of children watching their parents dying, their families suffering, their older brothers being hauled off in the middle of the night to fight.

Maha was ten going on twenty-eight. As soon as I sat her next to me, she held on to her sister's hand on her right and touched my crotch with her left. I gently removed her hand and put it on her leg, making my action seem as accidental and thoughtless as hers. She moved her hand back to my crotch. I removed her hand again and laughed. I wanted to make light of a situation that I didn't understand.

It wasn't appropriate behavior for a child her age, but I didn't want to shame her.

"I think you're not being careful where you're putting your hand," I said.

"Why?" she asked. "Don't you like me?"

I explained to her that she was a very nice girl but that when people liked each other they could simply hug.

"Like this," I said and I gave her a hug.

There was a look of genuine incomprehension on her face. I looked at her sister. Her sister looked straight ahead. With one hand she held her sister's, with the other she sucked her thumb.

"How old is your sister?" I asked Maha.

"Myriam is seven," she said. "She's always holding my hand. Even when I'm working. There's no one else to take care of her."

"Even when you're working?" I tried hard to tone down the surprise in my voice. I knew better than to ask about the whereabouts of her parents. Besides, I wasn't sure I was ready for another incredible explanation. Maha volunteered the information all by herself.

"My father ran away, and my mother's dead. My grandfather killed her."

"Your what killed her?"

"My grampa. My jeddo."

I had heard all different kinds of stories from the kids at the camp, most of them involving some kind of violence. Some involved drugs, beatings, and neglect. But this was a whole new level for me. Here was this ten-year old who insisted on feeling me up while telling me that her grandfather had killed her mother and that she was, I assumed, a prostitute. And I had no idea what to do with this info. I needed someone to talk to. I needed Lana. I needed Jeddo. I needed Marc. I needed my mother. I needed something familiar. I needed to get out of this nightmarish place and this nightmarish situation that only seemed to get worse every day. I needed this to end. I needed to wake up in my bed, in my room, in my home, to go to my school, see my friends, eat kibbe and tabbouleh instead of corned beef sandwiches and lentils!

I told Maha I needed to check on something and would be right back. I asked her if she would like to color while she waited. I distributed paper and coloring pencils to the kids and asked them to draw until I returned. I wanted to go check on Lana. I wanted to tell her about my conversation with Maha. I wanted to tell her about my conversation with the director. I walked to her tent and peered through the opening. She was lying down on her cot with her eyes closed.

"Lana?" I whispered. "Lana, are you sleeping?"

She didn't answer.

I tiptoed inside and approached her cot.

"Lana?"

She moaned.

"Are you okay?"

She moaned again.

"Shall I come back and check on you later?" I asked. She didn't answer, and I didn't want to bother her, so I just left, thinking I would check on her later. Later, I would regret that decision.

Layla

She patted herself down. She was still wearing her clothes from the night before. She looked at the unfamiliar surroundings and tried to figure out where she was. This had been happening often lately. She wasn't particularly perturbed by the fact that she didn't know where she was, since she had often woken up in unfamiliar rooms and unfamiliar beds. Being dressed meant that at least she didn't have to figure out who she was with. She closed her eyes again. Her head felt very heavy, and her body felt mangled. She dozed a bit, then woke again and decided that if she wanted to figure out where she was, she had to get up and go through the door. She could smell coffee brewing. That seemed like a good sign.

She walked unsteadily to the door. She still felt a little dizzy. The door was a white, French-style wooden door with a latch lock like the ones she remembered from her youth. It was very tall, in a high-ceilinged room that, except for the cot and a mattress, was bare. Layla opened the door onto an open area. The first things she noticed were the beautiful brown and beige cement tiles on the floor. She was in a typical traditional Lebanese house but still had no idea where the house was located. In the middle of the room a group of people were sitting around a makeshift table on cement bricks. They were eating olives with fresh thyme and bread and sesame seeds. Marc was sitting with them.

"Good morning!" shouted Hisham. He held up a piece of bread in the air. "Look what we managed to find this morning. Come. Please. Join us."

Layla was surprised to see Marc sitting at the table and a little confused by the look of concern on his face. He was the only familiar face at the table. She sat down next to him.

"How're you feeling?" he asked.

"I'm fine," she said. She gave him her bravest smile, to hide her uncertainty.

"Sure?"

"Yes, why?"

Marc felt her forehead.

"Well, you're no longer feverish," he said. "But I suspect your body's pretty worn down. Why don't you go lie down a bit longer?" He helped her up. "I'll bring you some tea."

"Coffee," Layla said. "Please."

"I'll bring you some coffee."

"Thank you," she said. "Bon appetit," she said to the others.

She woke up some time later to find Marc sitting at the end of the bed.

"Hey!" she smiled at him.

"Hey," he said. "How're you feeling now?"

"Much, much better. What time is it?"

"It's around 10 o'clock."

"What?! It's so late! We have to go. We have to get Michael." She sat up in bed.

"Layla, wait. Relax. Maybe we shouldn't go. Not today."

"What're you talking about? Of course we're going today. We're going now!"

"You've been out for a few days. I'm thinking maybe you should rest a little longer. God knows what we're going to get out there."

"A few days? Don't be silly; that's not possible. I slept like a baby."

"Yes, you did. You woke up every couple of hours."

"No, I didn't! What're you talking about?"

"You don't remember anything? You really don't?"

"What're you saying? Remember what?"

"You've had a high fever for a few days now. A couple of nights ago you were hallucinating."

"Of course I wasn't! Look we don't have time for this, we must go."

"You thought I was Sebastian. You thought Hisham was your mother."

He recounted to her how she held his face in her hands and thanked him for coming to save her. And how she apologized to Hisham for not answering his letter.

"What letter?" Layla asked

Marc shrugged his shoulders.

Layla laughed heartily.

"I think you're the one imagining things now, darling. You? Sebastian?"

Marc nodded.

"Coming to save me? How can you save me? You can hardly save yourself!"

"Maybe it takes two," Marc said. "Maybe we're meant to save each other."

"Maybe." Layla stood up. "But right now the only person we're going to save is Michael. C'mon, let's go."

At lunchtime they finally got the all-clear. Layla jumped in the van like a kid going to Disneyland. Marc sat next to her with Hisham, and two other people jumped into the front seat.

"Let's hope we don't have to pick up anyone on the way or they're going to have to sit in your lap," smiled Hisham.

"Thank you," she said to Hisham. "I appreciate you going out of your way for us, I really do."

"It's what we do," Hisham said. "We help people in need. Different people have different needs."

"Can I ask you something?" Layla said. "Why do you do this?"

"Why do I volunteer you mean?"

"Why do you put yourself in so much danger? Don't you realize there's a woman out there worried sick about you? Have you no heart? No mercy?"

Hisham nodded and smiled.

"And there's another woman sitting here with me worried sick about her son, and I'm getting to help her."

Out on the road, the scenery looked like a monochromatic painting of grays and browns. Lifeless. The van bounded on rocks strewn all over the road by the bombing. Layla spotted a stray dog foraging, and her mind wandered to Miss D and her father. She wondered where they were and what they were doing. She felt the urge to put her arms around her father. He had looked so frail the last time she had seen him, and she regretted that she had been so harsh with him these past few weeks. He had tried his best and all she had done was lay blame on him. If she could just cuddle with him now, she would make a special effort to be kinder, to apologize, to tell him that she understood he had her best interests at heart. Marc reached out and held her hand, and she squeezed it back. And Michael. She was going to hug him close and not let him out of her sight ever again. But the thought that she wasn't going to be able to keep him for long, judging by one of their last conversations, kept nagging at her.

"How d'you know you're ready to go?" she asked him one time when he had alluded to applying to schools abroad.

"I'm ready," he said. He hadn't allowed her to distract him from the chords he was practicing on the piano.

"No. You think you're ready. No one's ever really ready."

He ignored her comment.

"Michael," she called him by his full name to show him she was angry. "I'm talking to you."

He moved on to a jazzy composition he was working on. "Maybe you're not ready," he said. He raised his eyebrows, and she wanted to slap him because she was so frustrated.

"What on earth prompted you to buy me a white piano anyway?" he asked.

"Don't change the subject!" she shouted. "And anyway, I didn't buy it." After a second of reflection she added. "It was mine."

He looked at her then, and he was so much like Sebastian in that moment that she had felt the need to hold onto the shelf behind her.

"Well, well," he finally said. "It's things-you-never-knew-about-your-mother time."

"This country is like Hotel California," she said. "Once you leave you can never come back. Are you ready for that?"

He started playing the chords to the Eagles song his mother had just referred to.

"I thought it's the other way around in the song. Once you're in, you can never leave."

"You know very well what I mean," she said.

"You came back," he said. During this whole conversation he had only made eye contact with her once.

"I had to. I had no choice."

"I thought you said we always have a choice. On a dark desert highway, cool wind in my hair," Michael had started singing.

"Right," she said through gritted teeth. "I see you've inherited your father's inability to engage when you're at the piano. So I'll just leave you to it," and she left the room.

Now in the van, she felt guilty. She knew she had played dirty by mentioning Sebastian in front of Michael. She noticed that his interest had piqued slightly at the mention of his father, but he didn't say anything. She knew it was wrong to mention Sebastian, but she had been angry and frustrated. She vowed to sit him down one day soon and tell him all about Sebastian. He deserved it. Dammit, she had so many people she needed to apologize to.

"Are you alright?" Marc asked her.

"I'm alright," she smiled back.

"I think we're almost there," he squeezed her hand again.

———

The barbed-wire fence surrounding the white stucco wall with a huge red cross painted on it jolted Layla back to the living room of her youth. Every Tuesday at 7 p.m., one hour after the local channels had started airing programs for the evening, she would sit cross-legged on the floor at her parents' feet and, together, they would watch *M.A.S.H*, the American series about a mobile hospital during the Korean War. It was their sacred night together; no one was allowed to make other plans on that evening. Her mother would prepare toasted ham and cheese sandwiches, salad and nuts and beer—Layla was allowed a soft drink—and they would sit and watch together. She didn't understand any of the jokes, but her parents would laugh, and she would laugh at their laughter.

She had forgotten about that particular routine from her earlier years. But the memories came flooding back as she stepped out of the van, feeling as if she had walked onto the set of *M.A.S.H* herself, minus Alan Alda and Loretta Swit.

Their driver Amin knew the guard at the gate, and they stood chatting for a while. Amin was telling the guard that it was quiet outside today, that the bombing now seemed to be concentrated in the Bekaa valley. The guard said that his cousin told him yesterday they might reach an agreement soon. But only after all the bridges between areas had been cut. Then they said something and laughed, but Layla missed it.

A hot wind blew from the southeast, and specks of sand flared up into Layla's eyes. She closed them and tried to capture the smell of the orange groves for which the south was famous, but the only odor she could capture was the stench of burning garbage. The camp was bigger and neater than she expected. She had expected total mayhem but was surprised by how clean the tents looked and the relative precision with which they had been placed. They looked like oversized mushrooms. She could see people walking around at the far end and felt her heart beat faster when she realized Michael was probably among them.

"And now? Can we go in?" she asked Amin and Marc. She lifted the stray hairs from her face.

"Now we go see Jan," said Amin.

"Who's Jan?" asked Marc.

"The director. The director in the container."

The white-painted container sat on large metal legs with another huge red cross painted on it. It was as if the occupants of the camp took no risk that they could be mistaken for anything other than the Red Cross. The few makeshift steps led into a surprisingly bright office. Big squares had been carved into the metal with white-painted frames and mesh to keep the mosquitoes out. A ceiling fan hummed a little too loudly, but the only air circulating was hot. Jan was a big guy with a bald head and a trim belly. He jumped out from behind his desk to greet them. He greeted Layla first with a firm two-handed shake and then Marc.

"You must be Michael's parents," he said. He gestured for them to sit. "Can I offer you anything to drink? Coffee?"

Layla, embarrassed to offend by declining the hospitality, looked to Marc to get them out of Jan's office and to Michael as quickly as possible. The director seemed to have caught on and explained that he had already sent Michael to get his things and that he should be with them shortly.

"Amin told me you've walked all the way from Beirut? I couldn't believe it! Incredible." Jan said. "You must tell me how you did that! I tell you when we're done with this war, I'm going to write a book about this country. You just hear too many wild stories."

"Do you think we could go see where Michael is? He couldn't have that many things; he only ever carries a backpack," Layla asked.

"Oh no, he didn't even have that when they brought him over," and then as if realizing they probably didn't know the state Michael was in when he arrived, he added. "We can go wait for him outside if you prefer. I just thought you might find it cooler in here."

"Yes," she said. "You're right. It is cooler in here."

Marc placed his hand on her knee to steady her leg and proceeded to ask the camp director about how they were faring and if he had any inside info on how long the war would last.

Layla watched them, the jumbled and incoherent thoughts in her head drowning out all external sounds except the droning of the fan. And after a while, the creak of a rusting metallic hinge.

———

When Layla saw Michael, she was shocked by his appearance. She couldn't understand how he had grown taller and thinner in such a short span of time. She was used to his hair turning even blonder in the summer, but what she hadn't expected was the fuzz on his cheeks and his chin. On her journey, she had lost track of time, and she wasn't totally sure what day of the week it was or how many days exactly it had been since she had last seen her son, but what felt certain to her was that the Michael who was standing in front of her was no longer a boy but a man. Michael looked almost exactly like Sebastian had looked at his age.

The second thing that shocked her was his smell. He reeked of a combination of sweat and sewage and stale bread and cheese. Even his smell had somehow amplified, had become more pronounced, more present.

Layla ran to him and threw her arms around his shoulders, but her son felt stiff, rigid beneath her touch. There was a time when he would nuzzle against her, twist and shape his body so that he could fit into every nook in her body, cover as much of her as he could, fill every inch of air between them. But not today. Today he barely put one arm around her waist and didn't even bend down to kiss her.

Layla took a step back and scrutinized her son, trying her best to hide her disappointment. She looked into his eyes for answers as to where her boy had gone and where this man had come from. But she knew, of course. She had been the same when her father had come to visit her that first time in boarding school. She must have had that same look, that vacant yet deeply sorrowful look, a look that was still processing all that it had witnessed and seen.

"How are you, my love? How have you been?" She placed her hand along his cheek. His stubble was itchy.

"I'm okay." He smiled back faintly and turned his gaze to Marc and only nodded to him. Marc nodded back.

"Right!" Layla said, trying to remain enthusiastic. "I'm sure everyone here is very busy, and we don't want to take up any more of these nice people's time, I think they've helped us enough." She clasped her hands together. "Should we go then?"

"It's really no trouble, Mrs. Cape," Jan said. "This is what we're here for. In fact, why don't you stay and rest for a bit? You just got here. Come to think of it, how will you even return?"

Layla, Marc, and Michael looked at each other in turn. Layla wondered if she looked as puzzled as they did.

"Well, I suppose we could take a taxi back?" Layla proposed.

"The roads are blocked, Mrs. Cape, as you know. And as you know as well, the bridges have all been bombed," Jan said. "I don't know by what miracle you got here, but—"

"Mom," Michael shuffled his feet. "I'm not going back with you."

Marc shot up from his chair, as Jan sank deeper into his.

"Nonsense," Layla said.

"Mom, I think—"

"This is not about what you think, darling—"

"Layla," Marc interjected. "Let him finish."

"No, I'm not going to let him finish! This is not about what he thinks or what you think!"

"I'm not a child anymore," Michael said.

"Oh, please! You're not a child? Let's not go there, okay? A man doesn't apply to schools in England in hiding; a child does. Running—"

"I didn't apply—"

"Running away is not the behavior of a child?"

"I didn't—"

"Just be quiet okay, Michael? Please? You are a child. You are my child, and you're coming home with me right now. Go get your stuff."

"He doesn't have stuff," Jan said. "I was explaining—"

"Fine, whatever, go get anything you need. We're leaving, and we're leaving now."

"Layla," Marc tried again. "Why don't you hear him out?"

"Marc, may I calmly and kindly suggest that you stay out of this?"

"Mom," Michael said, his eyes now full of tears. "In this camp, there are little kids who are only five and six years old. There are babies even! Orphans. These kids need me." He turned to Jan.

"Sir, please say something."

"Son," Jan said, "as much as I appreciate what you've done here, you are a minor. And without your parent's consent, I cannot keep you here."

"But—" Michael said, but Layla interjected.

"Alright, so that's settled. Let's go."

"Go where?" Marc asked.

"Mom," Michael said. "Come and meet them."

"Who?"

"The kids. My kids. The ones I'm in charge of. Come and meet them. Please."

"Michael," Layla approached him, "I'm proud of you. I really am. I'm proud of everything you seem to have done here. But this is a war, okay? Now I know what I'm talking about because I've seen war, and I've lived war, and I know war. And I need you to come home with me now so that I can keep you safe, because as your mother, that is my job and my number-one priority."

Michael returned her gaze.

"With all due respect, Mom, if you haven't seen these kids, if you haven't dug your hands in the rubble trying to dig them out, you've seen nothing."

"Go. Get. Your. Stuff. Now."

"I don't have stuff."

"Good. Then let's go."

———

Denial is a powerful thing. It helps the body cope with shock when the mind cannot reason. When Michael was still around ten years old, Layla dreamed she was dying. She dreamed that she was sitting in a doctor's office being told she had terminal cancer for which there was no cure.

"Of course I'm dying," she had said to her doctor in the dream. "We're all dying. You're dying, too."

"Yes," dream doctor had replied. "But you're dying sooner than you're supposed to."

Layla thought she would never forget how she woke up gasping for air, as the true meaning of what it meant to be dying sank in; the terrible, unequivocal, irretrievable sense of loss that she had felt. She wondered upon waking if Sebastian had known he was dying. There must have been that one moment, that one instant where he figured: "that's it." Maybe it was the moment the knife had stung him or when he fell to the floor. Maybe it was the instant before he took that last gasp of air. Or maybe he had died while he was still in denial. She hoped so.

Her mother had come to accept death. She said so in the letter her father had given her on her eighteenth birthday, the one Marc must have been alluding to. But Layla had always thought that she couldn't have. Her mother was a believer. She said that she was not afraid of joining what she insisted was a peaceful and joyful afterlife: An afterlife where she could be reunited with her past loves and wait patiently for her new ones. But how could she have accepted leaving a twelve-year-old daughter behind? No, Layla had always thought, there was no way her mother had accepted it. She must have lied. She must have pretended.

And yet, when Michael stumbled back into the container, sweating, breathless, his eyes red with tears and fears, when he said: "I'm not coming back with you," Layla instantly understood what her mother must have come to accept all those years ago. She saw that Michael was not hers to keep, that she had no choice but to let him go. Despite his haggard appearance, there was steely determination in his words that told her she had no choice about letting him stay. She understood now that his fate was not hers to control; he was not hers to protect. Her son, by some great cosmic interference, had been lent to her, probably so she could fully embrace and apprehend what it was to truly love and truly suffer. And now that same force was asking for him back. She had no choice but to relent. All she could do now was to try to protect her heart from totally shattering to pieces.

"I'm not coming with you," he said again.

"I know," Layla answered.

"Your mother and I were just leaving," Marc said. He put his arm around Layla's shoulder, and she was grateful for it.

"How will you go back?" Jan asked.

"The same way we came, I guess," Marc replied.

"We'll escort you as far as we can," Jan said.

Michael

My own behavior shocked me. I'd never spoken to my mother in that tone before, never stood up to her like that before. And poor Marc; I'd hardly even acknowledged him. Of course, I'd seen my mother like this before, on the verge of rage. Sometimes, I would back off. Sometimes she would, I never understood by what mechanism, instantly calm herself down. But I'd never pushed her this far, and I really felt she might reach out and slap me for the first time ever. But for the first time in my life, I also felt that something mattered to me more than my mother. For the first time ever, I didn't care too much to please her. I cared about Lana. I cared about my kids. I had spent most of my childhood worried about my mother and how she felt. I still cared about her, but now, compared to them, she seemed just fine, to be honest.

But she seemed adamant, and without her consent, I couldn't stay. Marc tried to interject, but she ignored his words. I had no choice. I had to go.

I felt rage, anger, pity, and numbness all at the same time. I felt as lost as I had on that first day, whenever that was. I had lost track of time. I couldn't remember if I'd been here a few days or a few months. I had no idea when I had transitioned from wanting nothing other than to get home to my mother to wanting nothing to do with her.

I stood outside my tent. I didn't know what to do. I didn't even know why I was standing in front of my tent. I had nothing here. They had given me everything I now had when I came. The red overalls, toiletries, t-shirts, socks, everything. Even the books weren't mine. I stared at my mattress on the floor. I should probably remove the sheets and give them to somebody to wash. I looked around me. Life at the camp continued buzzing. No one at the camp seemed to realize I was leaving—or maybe they didn't care. Either way life had to go on, with or without me. In that case, maybe it would be easier if I just disappeared without saying good-bye. Maybe that would be less painful for the kids. Maybe it wouldn't be too hard on Lana. Or maybe I was the one who couldn't handle it.

I walked towards Lana's tent. She should be up by now, and maybe she would be feeling better. Someone would've gone to see her and given her something to manage her pain. Maybe she could even speak with the director and explain to him why it was necessary that I stay.

But I walked in to find Lana lying very still in bed, and the only thing that told me she wasn't dead was that her face was bright red instead of blue.

"Lana?" I asked quietly at first. When she didn't answer, I tried a bit more loudly, until finally I was shaking her by her good shoulder. "Lana! Lana! Are you okay?"

Lana just moaned. I had to get help. I bolted outside and ran straight into Malek.

"It's Lana," I gasped. "I think she may be dying."

Layla

On her eighteenth birthday her father had given her a letter.

"This is from your mother," he said.

She stared at him blankly.

"She wrote it before she, um—"

"Before she passed away," Layla had helped him.

"Yes."

"And you've kept it all this time?" She asked. "Why didn't you give it to me before?"

"She said I should give it to you on your eighteenth birthday."

"And you've never read it?"

"No, of course not. It's for you."

"You've kept a letter with you for six years, and you've never read it?!"

"No."

"Wow. Such discipline! You're amazing."

"Aren't you going to open it?" he asked.

Layla had stolen a quick glance at the envelope and felt her throat constrict at the sight of her mother's handwriting. *For Layla.*

"Not now," she said and put the letter nonchalantly in her bag. "Now I'm sitting with you," and she had squeezed her father's hand.

In bed later that night, Layla had read the letter. It was not the letter of a dying woman but of one who was very much alive. Her mother had wanted to share with her daughter what her own mother had taught her about being a woman. *This is not a letter about how to die, it is a letter about how to live. In it, I address, not Layla my child, not Layla the girl, but Layla my daughter, Layla the woman.*

Layla had read and reread the letter. She cried silently, not at the reading of her mother's words nor at the sight of her handwriting, which had made Layla feel as if her mother had been with her in the room. She cried because as close as she had felt to her mother in that moment, she couldn't conjure up her face nor hear her voice.

———

The first thing Layla did upon returning to her home in Badaro was to rummage in her drawers looking for her mother's letter. She had forgotten about it. It had been relegated to the "before" lobe in her brain. Before her mother died, before she left the country, before she met Sebastian. Before, when she was a little girl, when her experiences still matched her age, when life was predictable and stuck to its course.

Her memories of the days following her mother's death were hazy. She couldn't remember exactly on what day of the week her mother had died, despite remembering every single other detail, like what she was wearing (faded baggy jeans, short pink t-shirt, black Converse All Stars and a yellow barrette in her hair) and what song was playing on the radio ("Somethin' Stupid" by Frank Sinatra) as her father walked in the door, looking like he had lost inches from the weight on his shoulders. But most of all, she remembered this: she had no idea what she was supposed to be thinking. Her body had felt very light, hollow. Her head, in contrast, felt heavy and full. What was she supposed to do now? Many years later, she would hear a line in a movie: "what do you do the day a loved one dies?" At least, she thought, she hadn't been alone in her confusion.

Now, in her flat, Layla couldn't recognize the woman her mother was addressing. Could her mother have guessed that Layla's life would upend itself? Of course not. Her mother had taken a pleasant, sweet, happy girl and transposed her into a future self. But she had kept everything else constant. She couldn't know. Of all her mother's exhortations, Layla had managed to keep only one. *Music*, her mother had written at the end of the letter. *Always music*.

Layla put the letter back in its place.

She poured herself a glass of wine.

She put a Steely Dan CD in the player and sat down on the floor with Miss D. She thought of Michael asleep in his tent. She imagined her father sitting with a book and a cognac on his balcony. She wondered if Marc was making love to a woman. She stroked her dog.

"I love you, Miss D," she told her.

Marc

Marc circled the block a few times before he finally parked his car in front of the traditional stone house. There were fewer and fewer old houses like this one. Those that had not been destroyed by war were being destroyed by property developers who knew they could get higher profits from fifteen-story concrete buildings.

Marc read the sign outside to make sure he was in the right place and walked in.

"I would like to report a missing person," he said.

The lady behind the desk told him that until the government took concrete action, all that the Committee of the Families of the Kidnapped and Disappeared in Lebanon could do was record the names of the missing and cross-match them with any lists they had of people confirmed dead. She took his brother's name and asked him to come back later that afternoon, only to tell him then that his brother's name had not appeared on any list and that his best bet, for now, was to try and track down some of the people his brother may have been with the last few days before his disappearance.

He wanted to tell her that he had already done that, that she was utterly useless, that this is exactly why he hadn't come before. Instead, he just thanked her and walked out. Just as he reached the door, she called him back.

"What day did he disappear?" she asked.

"The 23rd of August 1977," Marc said. "He was crossing over into West Beirut."

"At which point?" she asked.

"Sodeco," he replied.

"There's someone you may want to speak to," she said.

"Who?" Marc asked. "This guy they call the Syrian?"

"No. He's Palestinian, ex-PLO. He was commanding the Sodeco crossing that day," she said. "But someone from our team will have to go with you."

"Why?" he asked.

"Just to make sure you don't kill him," she said.

"I'm not going to kill him," Marc replied. "I have too much blood on my hands already."

The man he was sent to see was called Yahya Baroud. He was now in his seventies, with a full head of white hair and eyes that conveyed regret and sorrow. Repenting eyes, Marc thought. He lived alone in an apartment with little light and dusty furniture.

"I have chosen to live with the least light possible," he said to Marc. "And with as few people as possible. I have created my own purgatory."

Marc handed him a passport picture of his brother, and Yahya promised to find out what he could from his contacts. A few days later Yahya called him to tell him that his contacts in Syria had confirmed that his brother had been shot in front of a firing squad and that he has been dead for thirty years.

"There is not one day that I do not regret my actions, the suffering that I have caused," Yahya said. "But I know that Allah will give me the punishment that I deserve. I will add you and your family to my prayers."

"There is only me left," Marc said and closed the phone.

Layla

The next thing Layla did when she got back to Beirut was go see her father.

"You're very brave," her father said when she told him she had left Michael at the Red Cross camp. "That couldn't have been an easy decision, especially for you."

"I didn't have a choice, Baba. He ran into that container crying. His eyes were bloodshot, and he was crying like he used to when he was a baby. Yet, somehow, through his tears, I could see the man he had become, you know what I mean? Somehow, through his vulnerability, I could see his strength."

Her father nodded, smiling.

"Yes," he said. "I know what you mean."

"I'd somehow missed him growing up. When did he grow up?"

"He's a fine young man," Jeddo said.

"Baba," Layla hesitated before she spoke again. "I've made so many mistakes over the years. So many mistakes, I don't even know where to start fixing."

"They're not called mistakes," Jeddo said. "They're called experience."

"I never realized how hard it must have been for you. Without Mama, sending me away. Now I see how difficult that must've been. I feel like I've been in a bubble underwater all this time, not seeing much and hearing only muffled sounds. I'm so sorry if I've hurt you. I'm really sorry, Baba."

Jeddo stroked her hair.

"There's nothing to be sorry about," he said.

"Remember that letter you gave me on my eighteenth birthday? I reread it. I can't recognize the woman in the letter. Not Mama—me, I can't see the girl she's referring to."

"To me you've always been that girl. Sweet, generous, loving Layla," her father said. "You'll always be my little girl."

"Sometimes, I wish Michael would leave already, so I don't have to worry about him leaving all the time."

"You know what your mother always used to say? She used to have a black-and-white picture of this bird, a heart-breaking picture of this bird sitting on a fence with snow billowing all around it. The bird was almost completely buried under the weight of the snow on its back. She used to bring out this picture, I swear out of nowhere; it's like she had it hidden in her bosom, ready to use at any moment. It was her weapon. She would bring out this picture, and she would say 'You never know how strong you are until being strong is your only choice.'" Her father chuckled at the memory.

"And you know what I discovered years later? These were not even her words. She stole them from Bob Marley."

"Bob Marley? You guys listened to Bob Marley?"

"No woman, no cry," her father replied.

Layla smiled.

"And sweetest—in the Gale—is heard—

And sore must be the storm—

That could abash the little Bird
That kept so many warm—
"The stronger the storm, the louder the bird sings," Layla explained.

"See? You quote Bob Marley, I quote Emily Dickinson. And to think you're the professor." Layla tapped him gently on the leg, and he held her hand in his.

"I think, in his mind, Michael has left already," her father said. "But know this, no matter how wide he travels or how far he goes, no matter who he becomes, he will always be your son. And you will always be his mother."

That afternoon Layla took Miss D for a walk around the neighborhood. It was quiet, so she decided to walk towards the center of the city. She wanted to interact, wanted to soak up the energy, to feel, see, and smell the city. As she walked from her neighborhood past the French Cultural Centre and the French university, she could feel the air change. Every quarter in Beirut felt like a different city. Every area had its own architecture, customs, sounds, and smells. Maybe that's what made it so attractive and so repellent at the same time. Maybe it was that dichotomy that was so enchanting. At the French Embassy, hundreds of people were waiting in line. Many foreign countries had started repatriating their nationals, and all of a sudden half the country's dual-citizenship holders decided they were no longer Lebanese. They also wanted to be repatriated by their adoptive countries. Layla picked up her camera and started taking pictures. Later, when she developed her film, she noticed that despite the differences in outward appearance, the faces all wore the same uncertain look. Their expressions showed the same combination of hope and despair that only a country like Lebanon, with its promise of the best of times and the worst of times, could elicit.

Michael

My mother had been so excited. We were finally going to watch her favorite movie ever! She had put the blinds down, made popcorn, and even let me drink a soda. She had been giddy with excitement. But once my popcorn and soda were finished, I asked if we could watch something else. What there was to like about a bunch of kids wearing curtains and running around grassy plains and snowy mountains singing melodic songs, I didn't know.

My mother was livid.

"How can you not like it?" she gesticulated wildly. "It is, without a doubt, the best movie ever made! It won five Oscars!"

I shrugged my shoulders. I didn't know who or what an Oscar was. I didn't like the movie.

"Alright, no worries," she said, pressing the remote a little too emphatically. "That just tells me you have zero taste in movies. That's not your fault. Here," she said, handing me the remote control, "put on whatever you want."

I was seven years old.

The movie was *The Sound of Music*.

In the movie there was a scene where the kids are playing ball with their soon-to-be stepmother, and they are very upset. Their nanny Maria (Julie Andrews) had just left them and returned to the convent, and they were visibly distraught, taking out their anger on the very beautiful baroness, who, in fact, was the reason Maria had left in the first place.

Now imagine this scene, but with the baroness equally distraught. That's how life at the camp was for the kids and me with Lana gone. It wasn't the same without her. I missed her. The kids missed her. We felt like we were in a boat without a rudder.

Lana had been taken away to another camp up the road, one equipped with a better medical clinic, where she could be adequately treated for her sepsis.

"I think we caught her just in time," Malek explained to me after the commotion had died down. "A few more hours, and she would've died. It's good you warned us."

I'd been sitting in front of her tent waiting, for what I had no idea. After I'd warned Malek that she was dying, a whole bunch of people came running. I followed them into the tent, but they pushed me out. "Get him out of here," someone had screamed. I ran back to the container. I knew there was no way I was leaving that camp now. Eventually maybe, but certainly not now.

"I'm not coming with you," I told my mother.

And just then, in a tiny flash, I saw my mother for who she truly was, a beautiful, strong woman who seemed very, very tired.

"I know," she replied. There seemed no need for any more words.

"I have to run back," I said and left.

A short while afterwards, they took Lana away. They wouldn't let me back inside the tent—"someone get this boy out of here!"—and the only thing I could see was that she was being carried out on a stretcher. She seemed unconscious. I was pretty sure I shouldn't have listened to her when she told me not to let someone know earlier about her state. Now Malek explained to me that I may just have saved her life and increased her chances of survival, and I wanted to tell him that on the contrary, I may have contributed to killing her. I didn't say anything. I wondered if I should have gone back home with my mother. I wondered if I was strong enough for this camp, for this life. I wondered if I even wanted to be here.

With Lana gone, I was unsure about my purpose in being here. The lunch bell rang. I had to go make sure the kids in my group were eating. As I walked towards the cafeteria, something made me go to the entrance of the camp. I looked out, not sure what or whom I was looking for. Suddenly I felt like a prisoner, unable to leave and not even sure I wanted to go for fear of what lay outside. In the distance, I saw a dog tied with a chain to a shed. He was barking under the blistering sun. I felt utterly hopeless. Is that what it meant to grow up? To be hopeless? What about my kids? They laughed and played, and save for a few, seemed unable to comprehend how desperate their situation actually was. They seemed unable to understand that maybe living inside these barbed wires was as good as it would get. I wanted to run and free that dog. I wished I'd alerted the doctors about Lana's state sooner. I wished I'd hugged my mother before she left. I wished I'd waited in the container just long enough to say goodbye.

Marc

He drove to his parents' apartment for the first time since he had buried his father and moved to France. Jeddo was right; maybe it was time to stop running away. The building had been renovated since he last visited, and a lift had been installed. He took it up to the fifth floor and stepped into the darkened space.

The apartment was exactly as he had last seen it. Whoever had said that nothing evokes a sense of place like smell had forgotten about the bold patterns and strong colors of 1970s curtains and wallpaper. His mother had loved these patterns, had grown attached to the rounded edges and natural materials that made up their home furniture. When everyone started refurbishing their homes towards the end of the decade, moving to more neutral tones of beiges and mauves, to smoked mirrors and sharp edges, or to the bolder black and white tiling, his mother had stayed with her beloved pieces, most of which, like the Saarinen tulip table, had since become design classics. Now they just sat there waiting for no one.

He walked into the kitchen and was immediately cast back in time. He could see his mother and the second-floor neighbor in hushed conversation, he could hear their stifled laughs. His mother's nails were beautifully manicured and painted red, her hair *mis-en-plis*. For a long time, he had thought the French word for *styles* was a Lebanese word, *misanpli*, because everyone, from the grocer's wife to the ladies in the casino, had their hair done. Every neighborhood sported at least five to ten hairdressers to keep up with the demands of Lebanese women wanting to style, color, straighten, and defrizz their naturally curly hair. His mother's hair had been naturally blonde, her eyes blue, vestiges from the times of the crusaders in the 1200s.

"I'm European," his mother would joke often to his father. "You must treat me with respect, the way men treat women in Europe."

"You're Syrian," his father would joke back. "Count yourself lucky I'm not reporting you to the authorities." And then he would bend down and kiss the back of her neck. Theirs was a happy home. At least, until that fateful Sunday when a group of Christian militiamen, right-wing phalangists, stormed into their neighborhood and opened fire on a bus carrying Palestinians. That was the day historians would name as the spark that ignited the Lebanese civil war. But what academics often failed to mention was that the incident was only a spark. The engine was waiting to rev up at any moment.

He was surprised to see that the brown-and-green wallpaper had not peeled off. He opened the beige curtains whose geometric patterns had since come back in style. The windows creaked when he tried to open them, but by pulling hard, he finally managed to let the light and the air in.

Marc walked into the living room that separated the kitchen from the bedrooms. Unlike modern apartments, the living room was modest in size, but the bedrooms were large and airy. The living room had French windows that led out to a balcony. The blue velvet drapes he remembered had been removed, and only the valance meant to hide the curtain fittings remained. He stepped outside onto the balcony. The wicker chair was gone, but the iron frame of the swing remained. He had so many memories of being on that swing when it was still in their house in the mountains, where they would spend their summers as a family. Summers then were characterized by long lunches, walks after dinner in the cool breeze, and games of hide and seek with the other kids in the village in the house's many hiding places. The swing had been the only piece of furniture that remained from their mountain house after it had been robbed at the beginning of the war. Even the bathtub had been pulled out and the parquet taken out piece by piece. His father was devastated, but he had saved the swing. Now it was fixed in place by rust.

Marc surveyed the flats around him. Gone were the striped nylon curtains around the balconies that were supposed to provide a shield from the elements. Now people closed off the balconies with curtain glass, sealing themselves off from each other. Now, they would go into a lift and not say good morning. There was a time when each neighbor knew the news of everybody else, but no more.

Marc walked around the house, opening and closing cupboards, touching cups and ashtrays, caressing furniture as he walked. He walked into his bedroom. From the window, he could see the washing from the apartment across the street hanging over the balcony, just as it always had. It was comforting to see that maybe some things hadn't changed. He sat on the bed. It still creaked. He remembered how he had tried desperately to keep it quiet as he fantasized about the daughter of the neighbors next door and hid porn magazines under the mattress.

He left his brother's room for last. The bed was still made. The posters of Jimi Hendrix and the Beatles were curling at the corners, their colors faded. Marc leafed through the LPs, of which there must have been at least a hundred. He would take some with him and come back for the rest. He opened the windows and the curtains, lay back on the orange bedcover, and let the streaming sun warm his face.

Later that afternoon, he went to the cemetery and placed flowers on his parents' grave. It would be another eighteen years before he would manage to bring his brother's remains back and bury them with his parents'. He stood in silence. On his way out, he saw an old man at the other end of the cemetery reading a book. He seemed to be reading it out loud. Marc greeted him, but Jeddo didn't see him.

Layla

Layla decided to heed her mother's advice: "Don't worry about the future," her mother had written in her letter, "lest you have to live it twice." She hadn't remembered reading that before. *It's true*, Layla thought. There was so little she could control that trying to do so just seemed to push her deeper and deeper into despair. She would not think of Michael or of the bad things that might happen to him. Maybe, just maybe, bad things were about to stop happening to her. Maybe people whom she loved would not disappear from one day to the next. And even if they were to do so, she wasn't sure she could stop it. Her blinding anxiety was serving no purpose, not for her, nor for anybody else. James, that English guy she had met in Niha on that first day she went looking for Michael, was right. It was time she started taking pictures of the living.

Every morning, she would put on her white t-shirt and cargo pants, pull her hair back and up in a bun, put on sunscreen, grab her camera and Miss D, and walk out.

She took pictures of whole families living in entrances of buildings, pictures of deserted streets and leaflets thrown by the Israeli air force urging inhabitants of the city to flee their homes before they got blown to smithereens. *And go where?* she thought. She walked to the port and took pictures of people waiting in line to board ships. It seemed that every day the lines grew longer. People argued with personnel to allow them to take relatives, family members, and pets. Everyone had the same look, those who got on the boat and those who were turned away. They all had the same desolate look of uncertainty.

Layla would spend every evening in her darkroom, sometimes developing pictures well into the early hours of the morning. Within just the first few days she had so many she had to stack them outside.

But she knew these were not the real pictures. The truth was in the southern suburbs. That's where the bombing in Beirut was taking place. That's what she would need to document. Getting there by car was impossible, though, because all roads were still blocked. Roads that had not been ripped open by the bombing were manned by police. But it wasn't far to walk from her apartment. She would have to walk again, alone. She couldn't tell anyone. Her father would probably tell Marc, and Marc would physically restrain her if he had to.

As she packed the surrender flag she had fashioned by attaching a white t-shirt to a broomstick, she smiled to herself. She was behaving just like Michael had. She asked Mrs. Kamel if she could take care of Miss D just for the day, so the dog wouldn't be home alone. Just in case.

She hung the flag from her backpack and walked.

Getting to the southern suburbs was relatively easy. The streets were deserted, and it was a relatively short walk, under an hour. The country had been fractured into different pieces, areas that were so close to each other in distance yet torn apart by circumstance. While some waited at the ports and land borders trying to leave, others, just a few miles further south, were sheltering from bombs. Still others, a few miles further east, were partying, oblivious to the calamity all around them. And then there were those who, helpless like her, searched to make sense of it all the only way they knew how.

She was irresistibly drawn to the destruction. She took pictures of pieces of furniture strewn across empty lots, dolls and toys that lay dead to the world. She took pictures of burned cars. She took pictures of ambulances rushing in and out of the destroyed perimeter. She took pictures of young volunteers running to save lives under the bombing until one of them grabbed her by the arm and shoved her into an ambulance. He screamed something at her, but she couldn't hear him. His lips mouthed something to the effect of, "Are you totally nuts?" but she couldn't be sure. There was just too much noise and commotion to make sense of anything.

But the next day she found herself going back. And the day after, and the day after that. She would take pictures by morning and develop them by night until one day her father knocked on her door and without a word went around the house and confiscated every camera he could find.

"Maybe now you'll stop," he said on his way out. "I've already lost your mother; I won't lose you."

Her father had missed the camera she had managed to hide behind the television.

Jeddo

He climbed up the stairs slowly. At the sixth floor he stopped. It wasn't Layla's floor. She lived on the seventh. He checked his watch. It wasn't too early. He knocked at her door.

"She's gone," Mrs. Kamel said. "She left very early this morning with a broom in her hand."

"A broom?" Jeddo asked.

"I assume she needs to hang some kind of rag on it and use it as a white flag," Mrs. Kamel explained. "Shouldn't you send someone after her?" she asked.

His mind blanked. He couldn't articulate his thoughts, but images of Layla flashed in his mind. In one, he held Layla in his arms, in another her mother was changing her, and in yet another she was bursting with laughter and happiness. He held her hand, walked her down the aisle. She was a year old, ten years old, and now she was a grown woman. He realized that these were not just images flashing in his mind but actual pictures he had at home;

pictures that helped him document his life and make sense of it. Give meaning to it. Maybe he should not have confiscated her cameras after all, and evidently he hadn't found them all. Maybe he shouldn't have tried to stop her. Maybe this is what she needs to make sense of her own life.

"Nadim?" asked Mrs. Kamel. "Are you alright?"

"Yes," Jeddo smiled. "Yes I am."

"Aren't you worried she might get lost?"

"She's been lost for longer than you can imagine, Mrs. Kamel," Jeddo said. "At least now I know where to find her."

"She's very brave." Mrs. Kamel said.

"Maybe she just feels she's been running away from the truth for too long," Jeddo said. "Maybe we all have."

After an awkward silence, he turned to leave.

"Nadim," Mrs. Kamel hesitated, then said: "Since you're already here, would you like to come in?"

"Yes," he said. "Yes, I would like to come in."

Michael

Life at the camp was dull. Every day I tried to come up with new ideas and new activities to keep the kids entertained, but they had lost interest, and so had I. Every day I asked to go see Lana, and every day my request was denied. Every day I was given a different excuse.

She needs to rest.

She needs to stay isolated.

There's no one to take care of the kids.

Roads are closed today.

Two boys just got bombed off their bicycles.

It's not safe outside.

So I stopped asking. And the kids stopped asking me. Instead, they fought, especially the older ones, while the little ones took sides.

"Do you even know what you're rooting for?" I asked them. Shouted rather. Then I figured it didn't really matter. These kids needed to root for something, whatever it was. They had been uprooted violently from their daily lives, from their loved ones, from their security. It was normal that they would seek to plant themselves in the first droplet of water they found.

There were some kids my age or a few years younger that were not part of our group. They were being dealt with by nurses and doctors. Malek explained to me that they had other medical issues that had to be dealt with, and only when I pressed him did he concede that they were drug addicts.

"But some of them are only eleven years old!" I was stunned.

That's when I understood that in Lebanon we were not one people living in one place. I understood that in this country there were those who went to private schools and drove fancy cars and spoke three languages and travelled the world, and there were those who were subjected to daily incursions on their freedom to live, to breathe, to exist. There were those who had to resort to drugs, or worse, in order to deal. Marc and I had spoken often about the history of Lebanon and the war. These were common practices during the war. We had spoken of the contrast between areas and people, but somehow seeing it first hand was very different.

"Don't kid yourself." said Malek, "These stories are everywhere, not only here."

"But I'm not seeing them everywhere," I said. "I'm seeing them here."

Marc

She called him on a Tuesday at noon. It had been a few weeks since he had last heard from her.

"Is this a bad time?" she asked.

"No," he answered. He tried to muffle the surprise in his voice. "Never," he added.

She would like to see him, she said. Show him some of her work. She had been busy taking a lot of pictures. He knew that because he had asked Jeddo about her. After they had come back, he had given her some space. He hoped she would call him, give him some news of Michael. He missed Michael. He missed her, too. Michael had been his link to her and with him away—no news from him, Jeddo had said—his connection to her was lost.

At first, he texted her. Daily. Briefly.

How's Michael? Any news?

None.

You okay?

Yes, thanks. You?

All good.

After a week he stopped and started asking Jeddo about her and Michael instead. So when she called him that Tuesday at noon, he answered that he would love to see her work and asked if she would like him to come over or preferred to meet him somewhere.

"I'll come to you," she said.

She asked if he wouldn't mind her bringing Miss D with her, and he thought that was strange.

She had asked Jeddo about him.

"Do you ever hear from Marc?" she had asked.

"Yes," Jeddo had answered. "We speak a few times a week. He asks about you and Michael every time."

"How's he doing?"

"Seems fine. Why don't you give him a call?"

"How are you getting on with Mrs. Kamel? When are we going to have dinner together?"

But at 11:30 on a Tuesday morning, while watching the world through her viewfinder, it became clear to her that she didn't want to live without Marc in her life. She realized, during Michael's absence, that maybe she had always been using her son as the link between them. She had never resented Marc's presence, because he was always there "for Michael." When they had come back from the south, she wondered if he would call. He didn't. He texted. He asked about Michael first, and for some reason, that offended her. After all they'd been through together, she was hurt.

She was curt. Maybe that's why he stopped asking.

She was curt. She thought about all he had done for her over the years. Not for Michael, for her: picking her up from obscure locations, taking Michael to school and taking care of him when she couldn't, spending whole evenings with him at her house when she was out, walking down south with her for a whole week! These things, she realized, he had done for her, not for Michael. And what had she given him in return? She hadn't even gone to see him to give condolences after Jeddo told her his brother was thought to be dead. She was curt. She was busy "taking pictures." Too busy for her only true friend of the last fifteen years. Too busy for the only man, other than Jeddo or Sebastian, who had taken such good care of her, who had loved her as much as they had.

And she had loved him back, from the moment she had seen him extend his hand to Michael and introduce himself at her kitchen table. She had loved him silently, stiflingly, like a flame on a stunted wick that wasn't given room to breathe. And she hadn't needed to love him any other way because he was there for Michael. She hadn't even allowed herself the courtesy of acknowledging her love for him because loving him openly meant letting go of her past. It was letting go of a past she had fought so hard through, struggled through. A past that had taken so much time and effort to compose, construct, and curate. Loving Marc was letting go of Sebastian; it was letting go of her mother. It was letting go of Michael. It was letting go of the love, sorrow, and anger that had defined her for the last thirty years. It was letting go of herself.

Letting go of her past was like Beethoven throwing out the first fourteen versions of his fifth symphony. But the discarded versions had not been wasted, she thought. Instead, they had given birth to one of the most powerful pieces of music she had ever heard.

And so it was that at 11:30 on that Tuesday morning, as Layla took pictures of destruction and desolation, she figured it was time to discard this version of herself and build again.

Jeddo

ida, I think that stubborn mule of ours may finally be coming to her senses.

Marc

e came home from work and found her sitting on the stairs in front of the landing. She looked dishevelled. Her t-shirt was dirty, her face tan with dust and sun.

She smiled when she saw him.

"Don't ask," she said.

"What happened?" he asked. "Are you ok? Where've you been? Jesus, are you okay?" He knelt in front of her and checked her face closely. When the temptation to kiss her became too strong, he looked around for the dog.

"Where's Miss D?" he asked. "I thought you were bringing her with you."

"Can we go inside?" she said. "I'll explain."

Once inside, he asked her again what happened, but she put a finger to his mouth and shushed him. She dropped her bag on the floor, cupped his face with her hands, and kissed him.

Marc didn't dare move as she unbuttoned his shirt and took off her own t-shirt.

"I'm sorry," she said. "I stink."

Layla

She had planned to go home, shower, and grab her portfolio and Miss D before going to see Marc, but she had been standing a bit too close when the missile hit the building. The Red Cross picked her up again. They dropped her off in front of their Spears headquarters with the stern warning that should they ever catch her in the no-go zone again, they would make sure to leave her there. They took away her broom with the white t-shirt. Maybe it comforted them to do so.

She hailed a service car. As she was his only passenger, the driver was happy to take her to Badaro, but halfway there she asked him to take her to Marc's address. She needed to see him. The pictures could wait. Luckily, Miss D was with the neighbor again. Mrs. Kamel, after a lifelong attachment to cats, was learning to appreciate the wide-eyed, primitive affection and attention that dogs had to offer, and Miss and Mrs. were getting on famously.

Layla lay down on the bed and let Marc examine her injuries. He kissed her scratches one by one, on her face and arms and chest and abdomen. When he finally entered her, her whole body convulsed, and she swayed her hips to his gentle rhythm. She closed her eyes and let the warmth of his body seep through her.

After what felt like a lifelong journey, she was finally home.

They chatted long into the evening. He told her about his visit to his parents' house, and she told him about her trips to the southern suburbs. He made her promise never to go again.

"I see where Michael gets it from," he said.

"Marc," Layla hesitated, "when Michael leaves—"

He raised an eyebrow.

"You're letting him go to England?"

"When he goes to England, I was hoping you and I could, you know, spend more time together."

"What do you mean?"

"What do you mean, what do I mean?"

"What do you mean spend more time together?"

"I'd like you to continue being part of my life. And I hope to be part of yours."

"Layla Kazen, if I didn't know you any better, I'd think you were asking me out officially."

She blushed and laughed, a little too nervously, she felt.

"Maybe I am," she said.

"In that case," he kissed her forehead, "would it be too bold of me to ask you to spend the night?"

"I'd love that," she said.

When she awoke the next morning, she patted herself down. She was naked. Of course, she was. She smiled and reached across her pillow, but Marc must have gone out to check the news. She heard the murmur of the television outside the room. The clock next to the bed told her it was early afternoon! When she saw the date, her eyes smiled.

It was Michael's birthday. She must find a way to contact him today, to send him a message at least. She wished she could arrange to have a cake sent to him. Her little boy was sixteen today. He was growing up. Indeed, he had turned into a thoughtful and brave young man. She glowed with pride. As she reached for her phone, her thoughts drifted back to her lovemaking with Marc. She wanted to touch him again. She walked out of bed naked and reached for the door handle.

She heard her phone ping and the doorbell ring at the same time. She glanced at her phone and saw she had missed many calls from Michael and her father. She wasn't sure who was at the door, but the voice she heard from the other side shocked her.

"Hi, Marc," it said. "Is my mom here?"

Michael

nd just like that, it was all over.

The war ended as it had started, abruptly. Without warning and without consulting anyone.

As soon as I woke up, I noticed movement, a lot of commotion, and noise. People screaming to each other across the camp. Some were screaming not to, but at each other.

"What's going on?" I asked Kamal at breakfast.

"Man, where've you been? It's over."

"What's over?"

"The war, man! The war's over."

"What d'you mean, the war's over? Just like that?"

"Yeah! Just like that."

"Can't be," I said.

"Welcome to Lebanon. C'mon," he said. "We must go pack up. We're going home." He smiled, but I couldn't see what he was smiling about.

I saw Nurse Adla shuffling toward me ushering twenty kids in front of her. She looked like a geisha in a white coat.

"*Habibi*, the director wants to see you," she said, still funneling the children away.

"Nurse Adla?" I called after her.

"Not now, *habibi*, not now."

"You're going home," the director said.

"For real?" nothing was making sense to me.

"This time for real, son," he said.

"But, sir—"

"Son," he interrupted me. "We've been to hell and back these past six weeks. There's a lot do here today. Now, there's a bus leaving here at 9 a.m. I want you on it."

I felt like something was slipping away, and I couldn't stop it. I couldn't believe it was truly over so suddenly. I thought of Lana. I wondered how and when I would see her again. If I would see her again. And the children. I couldn't imagine life without these children anymore. As naughty and as difficult and as challenging as some of them had been, I had grown used to them. I had grown used to being around them, and now I had to pretend it never happened. Now I had to go back to an existence that did not include them, that did not include Lana. It didn't make sense to me. I wanted to scream and cry. I wanted to jump on the director's lap and hold his head with my two hands and shake him until he understood that, no, this was not over. But instead, I just said:

"I'm not sure everyone made it back, sir."

"What?"

"From hell. I'm not sure everyone made it back. I think some people are just getting there."

I'd decided it would be less painful not to say goodbye to the kids. I stood at the entrance gate to the camp waiting for the bus. I was free to go, but I wasn't sure I wanted to. The dog was still chained to its house across the road. Part of me wished I could be tethered to a doghouse too. I wished I didn't have to make decisions. I wished I couldn't see and feel what I had just experienced. I wished that my heart didn't have to ache so much. I wished that I didn't have the option to leave this murderous place that only seemed to know how to kill people and their hopes and dreams. I wished that I didn't have the option to turn my back on everyone. I wanted to stay. I stared back at the dog.

"Freedom's overrated, buddy," I said.

I heard feet running behind me. I turned around to find the kids running over. Hussain, Maha dragging her sister behind her by the hand, Karina, Ahmad.

"Micol! Micol!" they ran to me. I knelt down and opened my arms wide. For me, this war had ended, but for these children, it was just beginning. This is what it meant to be a child of this country. It meant loss and pain and suffering. It meant breathtaking views and crisp weather and delicious food and heartache. I vowed to myself that I would never forget these kids.

These are the dots Jeddo always used to talk about.

"God gives us life in dots," he always told me. "It's up to us to join them. Life is never given to us complete; we are given it in bits and pieces. It's up to us to close the circle." No family in the south will be complete after this war. This is what it meant to be a child of this country. It meant separation.

In the last six weeks, I had probably seen more than the average sixteen-year-old should see. I had experienced more than some people would experience in their whole lives. And I had understood what it was like to be powerless, powerless in the face of mighty strength. The whole world watched as people were uprooted from homes that had been razed to the ground. The international community looked on while thousands of people lost their lives, many of them women and children. The Lebanese themselves had again turned their backs and stuck their heads in the sand. They did not want to see this. This was not their war. But for others, whose only fault was to have been born on the wrong side of the Litani river, this war was far from over. For many of them, the horror was just beginning.

I understood why Jeddo wanted me to leave. He did not want me to live in a country that hit pause and rewind every few years; he did not want me to witness what I had just witnessed. But it was too late.

I had set out to prove to my mother that I was a man, that I was old enough to be on my own, to take care of myself, but maybe she was right. Maybe I was just a boy; maybe I wasn't yet ready to be a man. I understood why she didn't want me to go. She had grown up too quickly, she said. Maybe I didn't have to, but now it was too late for that too.

"Hey," Boulos patted me on the shoulder. "I hear you're going home. Good for you. Take me with you."

"What happens now, Boulos?" I asked.

"Now," he sighed. "The big guys take over."

"It's weird not to hear the constant hum of the planes," I said. "I feel like I should expect planes to bomb any second."

"It's a weird place," he said. "But what can you do? It's home."

"What's the date by the way?" I asked.

"August seventeen," Boulos said.

My birthday.

Layla

The dried pine cones crackled under Layla's feet as she walked towards her mother's grave. She loved the pine trees in this place. She never thought of them as trees, more as protectors, their long slim trunks rising majestically into a tuft of needles that nevertheless billowed in the breeze. She had carved her name on many of these trees. She checked them now for the heart she had carved so long ago. It was still there. An arrow shot through it with an L on one side and an A on the other. Aida. And Layla.

"What are you looking for?" asked her father.

"Nothing," Layla said, tracing the heart with her finger. She went to stand by her father's side and put her arm around his waist. One day he too would be gone, and she wanted to be able to remember the feel of him. She read somewhere once that one's longest relationship was with one's siblings. Sibling relationships were longer than relationships with one's children or parents, with whom one experienced only part of their lives, growing up without the first and growing old without the second. Siblings, unlike parents or children, were lifelong companions, the article had said.

"At least when they didn't face a shooting squad," Marc had commented.

Layla had no siblings, so she would have to reconcile herself to transient relationships all her life. She pulled her father closer to her.

———

Only a few days before she had stood at Sebastian's grave.

"I'd forgotten how beautiful it is here," she said to Michael, as they walked back to the manor. The ocher leaves were still falling lazily from the trees, seeming to languish in the gentle breeze.

"Your father and I got up to so many naughty things here; one day maybe I'll tell you about them."

"Please, don't," Michael said and squeezed her arm. Then he hugged her.

"I'm sorry I'll be missing your exhibition," he said.

"It's okay," Layla replied. "I'm glad Lana is coming to visit. It was nice of Adele to invite her. Besides, I plan on having many more."

He squeezed her a little tighter.

"I'm going to miss you so, so much, Mama," he whispered in her ear. "Thank you. For everything."

"Don't you dare," Layla said. "Don't you dare make me cry."

But it was too late.

They walked the rest of the way in silence. At the house, Layla found her taxi waiting outside the entrance. She went into the house and kissed Adele goodbye.

"Take good care of him," Layla had told her.

"You are always the most welcome here, Layla," Adele said. "This is your home, too."

Layla promised to come back with Jeddo and Marc in a few weeks, but who knew? Who ever knows? *Inshallah,* the Arabs said. God willing.

On the dual carriageway, Layla looked at the majestic oak trees that lined the road. Summer was over in Cambridgeshire. In Beirut, it would be hot well into November. With any luck, it would start raining soon, and the stale scent of smoke that had been lingering over Beirut since the end of the war would start to wash away. And with it, people's memories would start to cleanse, and they would stop talking about the war. The Lebanese were really good at forgetting, perhaps because they had to be. Maybe it was this resilience that made them so dangerous. Layla dipped into her handbag and took out the photo album Adele had offered her all those years ago. This time she had taken it. This time, she promised herself, she would not forget.

There was something oddly comforting about saying goodbye to Michael, the familiarity: the hollowness in the gut, the emptiness in the heart, the heaviness of the chest. They were feelings she knew well. Her younger years had been punctuated with goodbyes, mostly "au revoir," as the French said, which translated to *until we meet again.* The exception was her farewell to her mother, to whom she said "adieu": to God.

In saying goodbye to Michael, Layla could ponder feelings she could make sense of, even if she never came to understand the circumstances that led her there. It was the luck of the draw. She had been born on this tiny portion of land, and to these specific coordinates she would always be bound. The Lebanese liked to joke that when God created the perfect country, a land of rivers and mountains and sea and sand, where the sun shone brightly most of the year, where the balmiest of breezes blew, where orange groves and apple orchards populated the coastal and mountainous lands, the closest representation of Eden on Earth, he had to give it a flaw to protect it from evil eyes. The flaw, the joke went, was in its location, amidst older, jealous siblings, who each wanted a piece of the pie, and with a population that, unable to appreciate the goodness given to them by a very generous God, angered him by not being content with what they had and protecting it with their utmost being, but instead pettily offered themselves and their country to the highest bidder.

This is what it was to be Lebanese. To be offered the perfect place and, through ignorance or greed or both, to want more. Perhaps it was living by the sea and all the opportunities it promised that made them greedy. Perhaps it was the contrast of the vast openness of the sea with the narrowness of the land. For all its perfection, Lebanon was small. It was fifteen times smaller than most European countries. But Lebanon, like the Lebanese themselves, had a big ego.

"We live by the size of our shadow," she had always heard Jeddo say. "Never truly committing to our real size."

Unable to accommodate all the people who loved it, the country had, since ships were first built, said goodbye to its best and brightest and bravest. Curiosity and a sense of adventure, a need to see, to check for themselves if they had indeed been given the best piece of country on Earth, drove many Lebanese to other shores. Only later would they discover, much to their chagrin, that they had indeed been too greedy, that nowhere else on this rock in space rivaled their own home. But by then it was too late. Because of its small size, there was no place left for those who had vacated theirs.

Layla had been one of those people, except it had not been a choice. All these years, she had blamed her father for driving her out, for giving her seat to someone else. At eighteen, when she had finished school, she had already, unbeknownst to her, become infused by foreign sensibilities. She could not see it, but her father could. When she told her father she was thinking of applying to the American University of Beirut where her father was a professor, he had told her to think again.

"Forget about this country, Layla," he said. The war had been at its apogee then.

"This country does not deserve you. You are better than this. You are still full of dreams, and dreams cannot be fulfilled here."

And she had tried. Truly tried. She applied to university in the UK, her adopted home. She met Sebastian, and for a while she had forgotten. She had understood, at that time, that there would always be two people living within her: the Lebanese dreamer and the English achiever. And she decided, for survival purposes, not only to feed the English one more but to starve the Lebanese one, to kill it. She wanted it out, gone, obliterated, vanished, with all the hurt that it brought with it.

After Sebastian's death, she had starved her whole body, literally and figuratively. That is when the Lebanese woman within her proved more resilient, more adaptive. It was at first teasing, then cajoling, then outright pulling her back towards a land she had become too tired to say goodbye to; she had been too weak to resist. But on returning to Lebanon, she realized that she had lost not only her place but her dreams.

She hadn't wanted Michael to feel the disappointment, the constant push and pull of a place at once magical and repulsive that she had experienced. She had clung to him to protect him from these feelings. Only now did she understand that it had never been up to her anyway, just as it hadn't been up to her father to protect her. Lebanon was like a dog: you didn't choose it; it chose you. It let you think you were in control while working its way into your heart. In fact, you were not in control, you were in the thrall of something that was impossible to comprehend, let alone steer. But it was an unpredictable dog, and if you were not always on your guard, it would jump up and bite you, scar you for life.

Lebanon had rejected Michael, just as it had rejected her. Like her, Michael would have to live in a state of perpetual goodbyes. And like her, he would have to accept this new state of being until it became his comfort zone. But unlike her, he did not seem to be building a hard protective shell around himself.

"We have to relieve those who love us of their burden," Jeddo said.

"I miss her," Layla said. "I miss her so much."

"Me too," he said.

They stood in silence.

"You remember that poem you recited the other day? What was it called? Something about a bird singing in the storm?" Jeddo asked after a few minutes.

"And sore must be the storm/ that could abash the little bird/ that kept so many warm." Emily Dickinson. How did you remember that?"

Jeddo squeezed her hand.

"It's time for you to sing again Layla."

A crunching noise told them someone was approaching.

"Hey, you," Layla said.

"Hi," Marc said and bent down to kiss her.

Layla's father spoke next.

"I'm sorry again about your brother Marc; how are you doing?"

Marc smiled at him.

"Closure," he said.

"Yes," Jeddo said. "You can stop being so busy now."

"Who's hungry?" Layla asked. She turned to her father. "How about we go grab a bite with Mrs. Kamel?"

"Come over," Jeddo said. "We'll open a bottle of wine on the balcony."

"I'll bring the pistachios," Layla said.

As the three of them walked out of the cemetery, Layla interlaced her arms with her father's and Marc's. From a distant balcony, she could hear a piano playing.

The End

History of Lebanon
A Timeline

SEPTEMBER 1920 Creation of the State of Greater Lebanon, under French mandate, out of the provinces of Mount Lebanon, North Lebanon, South Lebanon, and the Bekaa.

MARCH 1943 An unwritten National Covenant based on a 1932 census distributes power between Lebanon's three main religious communities Maronite Christians, Sunni Muslims, and Shia Muslims.

JANUARY 1944 Independence.

APRIL 1975 Phalangist gunmen ambush a bus in the Ain-al-Remmaneh district of Beirut, killing twenty-seven of its mainly Palestinian passengers in retaliation for a prior attack on a church in the same district. The fighting escalates to a civil war.

1978 Israel launches a major invasion of southern Lebanon. It withdraws from all but a narrow border strip manned by the South Lebanon Army (SLA)—a militia allied with Israel and composed primarily of Lebanese Christians fighting against other militia groups in the area.

JUNE 1982 Israel launches a full-scale invasion of Lebanon.

RANA HANNA

OCTOBER 1982   Foundation of the Committee of
the Families of the Kidnapped and Disappeared
in Lebanon.

FEBRUARY 1985   Most Israeli troops withdraw from the
south, apart from the South Lebanon Army.

OCTOBER 1989   The Lebanese Parliament meets in
Taif, Saudi Arabia, to endorse a Charter of National
Reconciliation. Power is redistributed among the
three main factions. The Taif Accord, as it is more
commonly known, made no mention of the fate of the
disappeared during the fifteen-year civil war.

OCTOBER 1990   The Syrian air force attacks the
Presidential Palace at Baabda, formally ending the
civil war. One hundred and fifty thousand people
are believed to have perished during the war, which
also caused severe displacement of the population.
The whereabouts and fate of 17,000 people are
still unknown.

MAY 1991   The National Assembly orders the dissolution of
all militias. The powerful Shia group Hezbollah refuses
to disarm. The SLA also refuses to disband. According
to the Committee of the Families of the Kidnapped and
Disappeared, the militias were disbanded "without
being constrained to provide any information about
the persons they had kidnapped or release any
prisoners they may be holding."

APRIL 1996   Israel launches Operation Grapes of Wrath
against Hezbollah bases in southern Lebanon,
southern Beirut, and the Bekaa Valley. A United
Nations base at Qana is hit, killing over 100 displaced
civilians.

MAY 2000   Collapse of the SLA. Israel withdraws its troops
from southern Lebanon more than six weeks ahead of
its July deadline.

FEBRUARY 2005   Former Prime Minister Rafik Hariri,
along with twenty-two other victims, is killed by a
massive car bomb in Beirut. Calls for Syria to withdraw
its troops intensify (Cedar Revolution) until its forces
leave in April. Assassinations of anti-Syrian figures
become a feature of social and political life. One
member of Hezbollah was convicted *in absentia* in
an international Special Tribunal for Lebanon. He
remains at large despite being sentenced to life
imprisonment.

JULY-AUGUST 2006   Israel attacks after Hezbollah
kidnaps two Israeli soldiers. Over 1,000 people are
killed, and over 4,000 are injured. Major damage to
civilian infrastructure in the thirty-four-day war
costs the country over three billion US dollars. A UN
peacekeeping force deploys along the southern border,
followed by Lebanese army troops for the first time
in decades.

AUGUST 2010   Foundation of the Act for the Disappeared
(ACT), a Lebanese human rights association whose
mission is "to contribute to the clarification of the fate
of the disappeared and missing in Lebanon, to foster a
sustainable reconciliation process, and to prevent the
recurrence of violence in the country."

OCTOBER 2019   Mass protests bring down the government
of Prime Minister Saad Hariri, son of Rafik Hariri,
paving the way for a transitional technocratic
government with the mandate to reverse economic
stagnation and political discord.

AUGUST 2020 A massive explosion rocks the port of Beirut, one of the largest non-nuclear explosions in history, causing over 200 deaths and over 6,000 injuries and triggering the third largest wave of emigration from the country. No one has yet been convicted of the crime.

OCTOBER 2023 Hezbollah declares Lebanon as a support front to Hamas in its war against the Israeli state.

SEPTEMBER 2024 Israel launches massive airstrikes on Lebanese territory in retaliation for Hezbollah's support of the war in Gaza leading to the killing of over 2,400 people and the displacement of over 1 million civilians from the South.

DECEMBER 2024 The fall of the Asad regime in Syria reveals the full atrocities carried out at the Sednaya prison located near Damascus and notorious for its human rights abuses. Following its opening by rebel forces, many detainees were freed but thousands remain missing. The press reported finding decomposed bodies, mass graves, and acid rooms.

About the Author

Rana Hanna was born in Beirut, Lebanon and was educated in France and the UK. She holds a Joint Honours in Politics and History from the University of Nottingham and an M.Phil. in Modern Middle Eastern Studies from the University of Oxford. Upon graduation Rana worked as a journalist at *Middle East Economic Survey (MEES)* and in management consultant firm McKinsey and Company. She was the editor of Deloitte's *Middle East Point of View* magazine for fifteen years.

Since emigrating as a result of the Lebanese Civil War, Rana has contended with issues of identity and belonging, specifically in Lebanon. When not writing, Rana enjoys spending time with her dogs and her adult children. She currently lives between Europe and Lebanon. *Birds in the Rain* is her first novel.

About
Bold Story Press

Bold Story Press is a curated, woman-owned hybrid publishing company with a mission of publishing well-written stories by women. If your book is chosen for publication, our team of expert editors and designers will work with you to publish a professionally edited and designed book. Every woman has a story to tell. If you have written yours and want to explore publishing with Bold Story Press, contact us at https://boldstorypress.com.

The Bold Story Press logo, designed by Grace Arsenault, was inspired by the nom de plume, or pen name, a sad necessity at one time for female authors who wanted to publish. The woman's face hidden in the quill is the profile of Virginia Woolf, who, in addition to being an early feminist writer, founded and ran her own publishing company, Hogarth Press.